MW00824522

The Wheel of Misfortune

A Psychic Suspense Novel

Cathy Peper

Gluesticks & Gemstones

Copyright © 2021 by Cathy Peper

All rights reserved.

No portion of this book may be reproduced in any form without written permission from the publisher or author, except as permitted by U.S. copyright law.

Contents

Chapter 1

P enny cut the cards for her morning draw, a ritual she had observed since moving to Little Hills. She drew the Wheel of Fortune. Considered by many to be a favorable card, it always struck her as ominous. What goes up must come down. She hummed the song by Blood, Sweat and Tears under her breath. The Wheel promised that those who were fortunate would go down while those who were unfortunate were uplifted. Fine, perhaps, if you considered yourself among the unfortunate. But these days Penny counted her blessings. She and her sister, Dora, might be just getting by, but things could be worse.

"Penny," Dora called from downstairs.

"Just a minute." Penny slid the card back into the deck and then placed her cards in their drawstring pouch. She shrugged off the reading. After an unsettled childhood, change didn't appeal. She had a job she enjoyed, and Dora was doing well in school. Their father was behind bars, which wasn't optimal, but at least he was healthy. She hated to think about her dad being in prison, but she didn't want him causing trouble, either. Of course, he'd proved he could endanger her even while locked away. Not on purpose, but because he knew some despicable people.

As she left the hobby room, she reminded herself that Ron, the former manager of the local casino, was also in prison, charged with setting off a bomb, which had injured several people, and kidnapping.

She paused, considering returning to draw a clarifying card, but Dora called her name again.

Penny set her shoulders and hurried down the main staircase and through the living room into the kitchen where her sister was eating a bowl of cereal, their dog, Plato, at her feet. She reminded herself she was not a slave to the cards. Everyone made their own destiny. The cards just helped make sense of things. "What's up?"

Dora set her spoon down and wiped her mouth with her napkin. "Can you get Sunday off? Julie's mom is coming to visit, and they have invited us to go to Faust Park and have a picnic."

Penny pulled up the calendar app on her phone. "Sorry, that's Mother's Day. The cafe will be busy. Can we make it another time? How long will her mom be in town?"

Dora picked up her spoon and began pushing bits of cereal around, but not actually eating any of it. "Well, here's the thing. It's a mother-daughter thing and you're more of a mom to me than our real mom is. I wouldn't want to ask her to come along even if we knew where she was."

Penny nearly dropped her phone. She set it carefully on the kitchen table and grabbed the back of the chair to help support her trembling legs. "You want me to go as your mom?"

"Forget it. Of course you have to work. It was a stupid idea, anyway." Dora shoved some cereal into her mouth.

"I'd love to go as your surrogate mom." Penny considered Dora's invitation a big compliment, but knew she had to tread carefully. Dora seemed eager to rescind the offer.

Penny grabbed a bowl out of the cabinet and started the coffeemaker. "What's the use of being assistant manager if I can't get time off? I won't be able to take the entire day, since it is a holiday and short notice, but if I help with breakfast and work the dinner shift, I can take off the middle of the day." The cafe didn't serve breakfast, but they prepared the food for Sycamore House Bed and Breakfast.

"Really? I'll let Julie know. We're going to tour the governor's house, ride the carousel and see the Butterfly House if we have time. The governor's house comes first since it's only open on certain weekends."

"Sounds fun." Penny felt a prickle of unease at touring a historical home. Her presence seemed to stir up ghosts. Or maybe Ben was the catalyst. He'd been with her at both Sycamore House and the Sunflower Showboat and was a talented medium. Since he wouldn't be going along on this Mother's Day expedition, she hoped she wouldn't leave with the memories of the governor, his wife, or anyone else who had lived in the old house.

"I gotta go. I'm meeting with the professor before class."

"Anything wrong?"

Dora shot her a look. "No, I just have a few questions."

Penny let it drop. Dora disliked her nagging about her grades her and her disability. She usually managed well with her hearing aid, but the university handled accommodations when necessary. Penny would fight for her sister if the university wasn't doing all it needed to do.

After the front door slammed behind Dora, Plato sat beside Penny and gazed at her with hopeful eyes. Penny sighed and patted him on the head. She couldn't resist his appeal. "You're so spoiled, but I guess I have time to take you for a quick walk before work."

Plato jumped to his feet at the magic word, his tail wagging madly.

"Let me just check my email."

Plato yipped impatiently.

Penny skimmed through the messages on her personal account, seeing mostly ads and spam. She then checked the email from her tarot reading website. The unease she felt after drawing the Wheel of Fortune card, and her constant worries about Dora, dissipated in a rush of excitement as she saw three clients had booked email readings. Her tarot business was growing.

The first client was a regular customer and the second a repeat, but the third name on the list was unfamiliar. She clicked on the new customer's profile. Clients signed up with a username and as long as they paid through a third-party site, could be anonymous. So, surely, her new client wasn't really the drummer of a popular band. No doubt he was just a fan and picked the name "DrummerHyperbolic" because it fulfilled some inner fantasy. An actual famous drummer wouldn't be reaching out to her for help, would he?

Plato yipped again.

"All right." Penny shoved her phone into her pocket. No time to investigate further. As soon as she took Plato for a quick walk around the block, she had to go to work. She had a contact in the music industry. Her friend, Juniper, was dating Adam Reed, lead singer of Out of Eden. Could he have recommended her to Hyperbolic's drummer?

She shrugged into her jacket and clipped the leash on Plato. The dog was dancing with excitement, and she wrinkled her nose at him. As she locked the door behind her, a grin spread across her face. She might have gotten her first celebrity client.

Maybe her world was turning—for the better.

Chapter 2

The rest of the week passed quickly. Penny completed her reading for her mysterious client. She was still unsure of his identity. He had asked for career guidance, but hadn't actually said he was a member of a rock band.

She'd been nervous about approaching Gage, her boss, to ask for time off on what was sure to be a busy day, but he'd approved her plan without hesitation.

To make it work, Penny agreed to help prepare breakfast, scheduling the woman who usually assisted the morning cook on the lunch shift. She also had a few extra part-timer servers and kitchen staff coming in to meet expected demand. She would be back from the park in time to work the dinner shift.

She woke earlier than usual Sunday morning and slipped out of the house without taking the time to eat breakfast. She would grab a pastry destined for the Sycamore House Bed and Breakfast.

Her jacket felt good in the crisp morning air, but only a few clouds obscured the sun, and there was no rain in the forecast. By the time lunch rolled around, she suspected she'd be ditching the outerwear.

The Carriage House Cafe was not yet open for business when Penny arrived, but their baker came in before dawn and the kitchen was already warm from the heat of the oven. Penny grabbed a cup of coffee, savoring the heat and caffeine as her nose filled with the scents of cinnamon and yeast.

"Well, what you waiting for? Come help me. These trays aren't going to make themselves," Rosa, the pastry chef, barked.

Penny took one last sip of the potent brew before tying on an apron and diving in. She rarely worked the morning shift, but knew better than to be afraid of Rosa. The older woman was short and round, with chin-length gray hair. Despite her years, she attended Riverview University, the same school Dora went to. Penny wasn't sure what she was studying.

She made delicious confections, and they were lucky to have her on their staff. Rosa worked six days a week, but only in the early morning hours. Penny hoped she would stay on even after she got her degree.

Penny followed Rosa's instructions, and it wasn't long before they had trays ready with pastries, breads, chopped fruit, and deli meats rolled into tubes. Penny also filled a large carafe with the cafe's signature coffee.

Brooke, the owner of the Sycamore House Bed and Breakfast, appeared just before seven in a modified golf cart with an enclosed compartment where the rear seat should be. The women loaded the trays into the space.

"Better go with her and help her unload," Rosa said. "Woman's about to pop."

Brooke's fair cheeks flushed red at the comment. "I would appreciate the help."

Penny climbed into the passenger's seat. She'd met Brooke when the woman first opened the bed-and-breakfast. Brooke had hosted a paranormal evening for the inn's grand opening, even though she didn't believe the urban legends about the house being haunted. Penny had signed on as a tarot reader.

However, the renovations in the house had released an angry ghost, looking for revenge. A greedy real estate agent murdered Brooke's husband and Penny's sister, Dora, had been possessed by the ghost. They'd only gotten the situation under control with the help of Ben, a local medium and photographer.

After her husband's death, Brooke discovered she was pregnant. She must be due any day now. Her belly protruded from her thin frame as if she were wearing a bowling bowl under her shirt.

"What will happen to your guests if you go into labor?" Penny asked as Brooke drove them the short distance to the main house.

"My sister came into town to help. She's going to run the place while I'm on maternity leave. I've only allowed my best customers to make reservations during May and June, so we're not fully booked." She pulled up at the back of the house, near the kitchen.

"I'll carry everything inside. You should get off your feet."

Brooke looked as though she might argue, but gave in with a weak smile. She collapsed into one of the kitchen chairs as Penny brought in the trays. Another woman, who shared Brooke's height and blond hair but was not as slender, bustled in.

Brooke introduced her sister, Heather, and then excused herself. "I need to lie down."

Heather thanked Penny for the delivery. "I can take it from here." Bacon sizzled on a griddle and a pan of fluffy, yellow scrambled eggs sat on the counter. Penny's mouth watered. Rosa hadn't given her a chance to steal one of her pastries.

She hurried back to the cafe where one of Rosa's scones awaited her, along with a fresh cup of coffee. Rosa had done her magic, tearing a swathe through the kitchen, and had left for the day. It would be Penny's job to clean up the mess so the kitchen staff could prepare lunch and dinner. She needed energy to complete the task.

An hour later, Penny hung up her apron and headed for home. The lunch crew would be in soon to prep, and at some point Gage would wander in. He still kept a close eye on operations, but had been glad to turn day-to-day trouble-shooting and scheduling over to her. It gave him more time to pursue his research.

Gage had confided in her that he was looking for a way to regain the remote viewing abilities he'd lost while working for a mysterious government agency. He couldn't tell her much about it, because of a confidentiality agreement, but she now understood why he buried himself under a mountain of paperwork.

But she didn't really relate to his obsession. In her experience, having a gift came with unexpected and undesired complications. If she were to lose her skill with the tarot cards, it would be a relief. Or so she thought. But when she recalled the excitement she had felt when she saw the user name on her new client's email, she wasn't so sure. Tarot added a lot to her life. She didn't just want to be held accountable if things didn't go as planned. Precognition and intuition weren't an exact science.

By the time she got home, Dora was ready to go. "They will be here soon to pick us up. Get changed."

Penny hurried upstairs and exchanged her uniform for jeans and a tee shirt with a sweatshirt pulled over the top. Layering was key to comfort in spring, but as she had predicted earlier, the day had warmed up to where a jacket was no longer required.

"They're here," Dora said, looking up from her phone when Penny came downstairs.

"Great." Butterflies flew around in Penny's stomach as they walked to the curb where a mid-sized blue sedan waited. She'd met Julie before, but had never met the girl's mother. To her horror, Dora joined Julie in the back seat, leaving the passenger seat open for Penny.

"Good morning, I'm Penny, Dora's sister,"she said as she slid into the seat.

"Call me Alice." The older woman turned a speculative eye on Penny as she waited for them to fasten their seat belts. "Julie has told me a lot about Dora. I'm so glad the two girls have become friends. But until this morning I didn't realize Dora lived with her sister. I assumed she lived at the dorms."

Penny wasn't sure just how much Dora had told Alice, but assumed her sister would not have mentioned their dad was in prison. "No, we live here. I've watched out for Dora since our parents split up and thought she might need some support navigating through college." She didn't even know if the older woman knew about Dora's hearing problems.

"Well, Dora is lucky to have such a devoted sister." Alice pulled out into traffic. Usually Sunday mornings were slow, but with Mother's Day and the beautiful weather, it looked like the historic district had drawn a crowd.

Penny suppressed a wave of guilt. The cafe would be fine without her. She'd been there less than a year and was hardly indispensable. She deserved some time off.

When Alice began quizzing Penny about her past, Penny moved the conversation to the present and turned the spotlight on Alice. She soon knew all about Alice's job as an office manager and a few details about her husband, Julie's father. She sensed Alice's curiosity about her own situation, but the woman was too polite to ask awkward questions. Alice seemed genuinely fond of her husband and daughter and appeared willing to extend her affection to Dora, Julie's friend. Gradually Penny relaxed. By the time they arrived at the park, she was looking forward to the rest of the day.

They toured Thornhill, the governor's house, first. The house had been built in the early 1800s and was the home of Frederick Bates, the second Missouri state governor. The state capitol at the time had been in Little Hills, although the government later moved it to Jefferson City. Penny wasn't particularly interested in early Missouri politics, but she liked old houses. The little old house she and Dora rented on Main Street had drawn her in so thoroughly, she'd abandoned her plans to live in a modern apartment complex with a gym and a pool.

Docents, dressed in nineteenth-century clothing, answered questions and showed how Bates and his wife and children would have lived during his short tenure as governor. Unfortunately Bates died less than a year after taking office. He was buried on the estate, along with his wife and one of their four children.

Penny didn't sense the spirits of Bates or his family, but that was Ben's area of expertise. She hoped that if they were present, they would stay quiet without him being there to act as a beacon for souls who had not passed on.

Dora seemed happy, chatting with Julie and laughing like a typical teenage girl. If she had trouble hearing the docents, she didn't seem to mind.

"I love visiting gardens," Alice said as they left the house and wandered through the grounds. "I'm not much of a gardener myself, but I can appreciate the work of others."

Penny murmured agreement, although she thought she'd done okay with the flowers she'd planted in the backyard of their house. As they reached the entrance to the cemetery, she hesitated. Stepping into a graveyard was more of a risk than she wanted to take. "I'm hungry. Should we grab a picnic table before they are all taken?"

Alice hesitated. "It should only take a few minutes to visit the graves."

"Why don't you go grab a table and we will join you there shortly," Dora suggested. She probably understood why Penny wanted to avoid the cemetery.

Penny agreed and walked back to the center parking lot. The main amenities of the park surrounded the small lot. There was a children's playground, a building housing the carousel, and a historic village comprising various structures moved to the park. The most popular attraction, the Butterfly House, accommodated hundreds of colorful butterflies.

Other picnickers occupied many of the tables, but she claimed one of the free ones, resting her arms on the wood and enjoying the warmth of the sun on her back. Kids played on the playground, shrieking as they slid down the slides and chased each other around the equipment.

Families wandered around the village, gazing at the exterior of the buildings since it wasn't open today. Penny made a mental note to come back when it was.

A few minutes later, the other three rejoined her. Alice gave the car keys to the girls and told them to go the main parking lot and bring back the picnic supplies.

"I'll help," Penny said. "You hold the table." She didn't want to be rude, but also didn't want to be left alone with Alice. When she saw the amount of food Alice had packed, she felt vindicated. Penny offered to carry the cooler, while Julie took the picnic basket, and Dora carried a bag of chips, plates, napkins, and plastic utensils.

"I ordered a variety of sandwiches since I wasn't sure what you liked," Alice said as her daughter began pulling food out of the basket.

Penny opened the cooler. Cans of soda nestled in the ice among water bottles, lemonade, and iced tea. Alice really had gone all out.

It was more food than they needed, but they had all worked up an appetite and they made a sizable dent in the contents.

"There goes my diet," Alice moaned.

"Relax, Mom, it's Mother's Day."

"Calories don't count on Mother's Day?" Alice asked, raising her brows.

Penny didn't think the woman had to worry. She was in good shape for her age.

"We could walk it off on the hiking trail," Julie said.

Dora glanced at her watch. "I'm not sure we have time for that. I want to ride the carousel and Penny has to work later."

"I'm feeling too lazy to hike anyway, but we could stroll around the village before checking out the carousel," Alice suggested.

They packed up the leftovers, and the girls took it to the car while Penny and Alice meandered over to the nearest building. They read the placard and peered through the windows, but couldn't see much.

"Dora says your mother abandoned you. It must have been very difficult."

Penny's throat closed. "Yes, I miss her a lot." Especially on days like today.

"I can't imagine a woman abandoning her children."

"My dad's not the easiest person to live with."

"Then she should have taken you and Dora with her when she left."

Penny shared this opinion and had often wondered why their mom left without them. "It would have been harder for her to make a fresh start with two young children."

"Sounds selfish to me," Alice said, low enough for Penny to pretend she didn't hear. She didn't totally disagree with the opinion, but it didn't really fit with the memories Penny had of her mother. She had always felt loved by both her parents. But if her dad was selfish enough to drag his kids along on his crime spree, perhaps her mother was selfish enough to do whatever it took to realize her own freedom.

Penny would even understand this line of thinking if her mother had come back for them once she got herself settled. She pushed the unproductive thought to the back of her mind, relieved to see Dora and Julie approaching. It didn't take long to walk around the rest of the buildings, so soon it was time to visit the carousel.

Dora grabbed Penny's arm and dropped a few steps behind Julie and her mother. "Remember how Dad would always take us to ride the carousel whenever the carnival came to town?"

"Sure." Their father loved it so much he'd ridden it with them long after they needed him for emotional support. Only later had she realized the crowds provided a perfect opportunity for him to brush up on his skill for picking pockets. He'd never been caught, and she didn't know if Dora knew about his reason for frequenting carnivals, so she kept her mouth shut.

"Someone always polished the brightly painted horses to a shine even when the rest of the ride was rusty and tired. The carousel here is hand-carved and beautifully restored to its original condition. It used to be in some old amusement park before they built the Six Flags theme park."

"The Highlands."

"That's it. How did you know?"

"I must have heard someone talk about it." Actually, Penny had read about it in a book on local history at the library where Juniper worked. Or used to work. Juniper was now on a leave of absence as she toured with Adam and his band. Penny had asked Juniper for recommendations of books to read, to learn more about her new home, but wasn't ready to admit as much to Dora. After years of living on the road with their father, the thought of actually having a home was too fragile and precious.

Dora squeezed her hand. "I wanted to come today because a carousel brings back happy childhood memories. And there were good times, as well as bad."

Penny squeezed back. "You're right. As usual."

Dora giggled. "Annoying, isn't it?" Then she dropped Penny's hand and skipped ahead to catch up with Julie.

Despite being forewarned, Penny's eyes widened at her first glimpse of the carousel. It was a genuine work of art and nothing like the run-down copycats she and Dora had ridden as kids. They bought their tickets and got in line. She was glad to see that they weren't the only adults riding without children.

When their turn came and she stepped on the platform, she felt a pinch of the old excitement. Choosing which animal to ride suddenly seemed important. She wanted one which went up and down, not one mounted to the floor. Where was the fun in that? And she wanted a horse, not a deer, although both types of animals were meticulously carved in vibrant detail. She chose a golden horse with a mane that almost seemed to move in the wind. It was so lifelike, Penny felt as if it was looking at her as she climbed aboard.

Dora chose a horse nearby, and Alice and Julie also found a spot. The old man who ran the ride checked everyone before starting it up. They moved slowly around, up and down, lights twinkling and music playing. It was a very tame ride, but Penny allowed herself a moment of nostalgic fun. Maybe that's why her dad had liked to ride, too.

A few minutes later, the music trailed off, and the ride slowed to a stop. As Penny slid off her horse, her hand caught on something sharp. She sucked in a breath as a jolt of pain shot through her palm and up her arm. She glanced down at her hand. Blood welled from where a sliver of wood had lodged deep in the meaty part of her hand beneath her thumb. Her head spun, and she swayed, falling against the wooden horse, who seemed to gaze at her with avid delight.

What on earth was the matter with her? It was just a splinter. Bigger and bloodier than usual, but still a minor injury.

The ride operator must have rushed to her side, for suddenly he was there in front of her. "Are you all right, miss?" He reached for her shoulder to steady her.

"I'm fine. I just got a splinter." Another wave of dizziness hit her, and she sagged against the horse again. Strange that she had picked up a splinter when the horse was varnished to a high sheen.

"I'm so sorry. It happens sometimes. Can I see?"

Penny curled her fingers, hiding the unusual burn scar that marked the center of her palm, but allowing the old man to see where the splinter still seeped blood. Nausea churned. Perhaps she'd eaten too much at lunch. She usually wasn't so squeamish at the sight of a little blood.

"I'll fix you right up," the old man said as Dora came up to them.

"What's wrong?"

"No need to make a fuss. It's just a splinter."

Dora winced in sympathy. "A nasty looking one." She turned to the old man. "You should take better care of the carousel. Not only can people get hurt, but it's a historical treasure."

"I know." The man bobbed his head. "I will check the horse after I see to your friend." He turned to the people waiting in line and raised his voice. "The carousel will be closed for about fifteen minutes. I apologize for any inconvenience."

"I'm fine. I'll tend to this myself when we get home."

"No, my dear, I must insist. You were hurt on my watch."

The nausea receded, and although she still felt unsteady, Penny stood straight, one hand resting against the horse for balance. It was cute—and touching—how the old man wanted to take care of her, but she'd been taking care of herself for a long time. "Thank you, but I'm fine."

"Let him dig it out," Dora said. "You're such a wuss about it, anyway."

Penny hesitated. Maybe she should let the man have a go. The splinter was in deep enough she probably wouldn't be able to get it out herself. She hated needles. "Well, if you don't mind..." Penny stumbled as the horse seemed to shift beneath her hand. Had someone restarted the ride? No, the horse was just drifting down, having come to a stop halfway down the pole. "Whoa," she said, giving the horse a pat on the head with her good hand. She turned her attention back to the old man. "I'd appreciate the help."

The man's eyes were wide with horror. His mouth moved, but no words came out, only a mangled sound halfway between a scream and a gasp.

"Sir, are you okay?"

The man clasped his chest, mouth still gaping, but only a ragged breath escaping. His eyes grew even wider as he crumpled to the floor of the carousel, striking his head on the platform. He flung one arm out to the side, his hand hanging limply in the air.

Penny screamed.

Chapter 3

D ora leaped into action. "Call 911," she yelled, kneeling beside the old man.

Penny fumbled for her phone as Dora began chest compressions. As she placed the call, Julie ran up to help Dora. Julie pinched the man's mouth closed and breathed into his mouth.

The dispatcher picked up. "Nine-one-one. What's your emergency?"

"A man collapsed. I think he's having a heart attack."

The dispatcher verified her location. "An ambulance is on the way. Is he still breathing?"

"I don't know. My sister and her friend are doing CPR."

"Are they trained in CPR?"

"I think so." Penny remembered Dora mentioning first aid training during one of her first weeks in school.

"Good. They should continue until the ambulance arrives." The woman continued to talk, her voice calm, but Penny was barely listening to her. After a few minutes, Dora and Julie switched places, but maintained their steady rhythm. It seemed to take forever, but eventually she heard sirens.

Minutes later, paramedics burst into the area, carrying a stretcher. They took over for Dora and Julie and started an IV.

"He's stable. Let's get him on the board."

The paramedics transferred the old man onto the stretcher. One of them placed an oxygen mask on the man's face and then spoke over his shoulder to Dora and Julie. "You did a good job, girls. You may have saved his life."

The paramedics wheeled the old man outside and towards the waiting ambulance.

"Wow," Penny said. Alice came over and gave her daughter a hug.

"I never expected to give someone CPR," Dora said. "Not until after graduation, at least." She took a deep breath and let it out slowly.

"No kidding," Julie said.

"You both showed real initiative," Alice said. "I think that shows you are in the right field. Unless you want to transfer into emergency medicine."

"No!" Dora and Julie answered in unison. Neither of them had moved from their position on the floor.

"I was so scared," Dora added. She held out her shaking hands.

Penny sat beside her and covered her sister's shaking hands with her own. The one with the splinter still throbbed dully and left a smear of blood on Dora's hand. Her sister noticed.

"I'll take care of you once I catch my breath."

"It can wait until we get home." The last thing Penny wanted was her sister poking at the wound with unsteady hands.

Alice drove them home. No one talked much during the drive, although Penny was no longer worried about Alice questioning her ability to stand in as a mother figure for Dora. Her sister and Julie had proved themselves capable young women, regardless of their upbringing.

Plato greeted Penny and Dora, tail wagging as if they had been gone for days instead of hours. The girls made a fuss over him, and he licked the blood from Penny's hand.

"Yuck," Dora said.

"I read somewhere that dog's saliva has healing properties." Still, Penny washed her hands before allowing Dora to extract the splinter. It hurt, and she wilted when Dora finally pried the small piece of wood free. Dora applied antibacterial ointment before topping it off with a bandage.

"I wish I could use it as an excuse to call off work." The physical and emotional toll of the day had exhausted her.

"Gage would probably let you."

"Maybe, but I couldn't leave him short-handed. I'll just dump some coffee down my throat." She changed into her uniform. Dora offered to give her a ride, but Penny declined and walked, since it was still a nice day.

The cafe was busy, but not insanely so, and her shift passed quickly. Tips were good and by the time they closed, she was glad she had come in.

After she and the other waitress finished setting up for the next day, she ducked into Gage's office. "I'm taking off now. Good night."

"We had a prosperous day. Want to grab a drink?"

Gage was her boss and had also worked with her on the Sycamore House and Sunflower Showboat cases. She considered him a friend, but they never hung out socially. Was he asking her out on a date? The idea wasn't as weird as she would have once thought. Gage was older than she was, but he was still a good-looking guy.

"Sure." She covered her mouth to hide a jaw-cracking yawn.

"What happened to your hand? Did you get hurt at work?"

"No, don't worry. I got a splinter at the park. No big deal."

"Big enough to bandage."

"It bled, and I allowed Dora to tend it. She's trained in first aid. In fact, she saved someone's life today."

"You look tired. Instead of going somewhere, why don't we share a quick drink here and then I'll give you a ride home. You can tell me what happened."

Not a date, then. He'd asked her out as a friend, or maybe a colleague now that she was assistant manager. "Okay." She slipped into the chair across from him and watched as he pulled a bottle from the bottom drawer of his desk, just as if he were a detective from an old black and white movie.

He poured them each a measure of amber liquid and slid a glass over to her. Penny rarely drank straight liquor, and she coughed after taking a sip.

"Lightweight." Gage downed his in one gulp.

"Guilty." She took another small sip before launching into the story of the carousel and the old man's heart attack.

"Will he be okay?"

"I don't know. The paramedics seemed to think he might recover."

"I trained in CPR, too, but it's been a few years. I should probably take a refresher course."

"It's a useful skill." As tired as she was, the alcohol was going straight to Penny's head. Not that she minded, since the stupid splinter wound still ached. Carrying platters of food all night probably hadn't helped.

"You look like you're asleep on your feet. I'd better take you home now." Gage guided her out the door with a hand on her back. It made her feel good. And safe.

"I'll do better next time."

Next time? Would there be a next time?

It took mere minutes to drive from the cafe to Penny's house.

"Need help to get in?"

"I'm not drunk, just tipsy." Penny stepped out of the car and waved goodbye to Gage. She felt him watching her as she let herself into the house. Too bad she had been too tired to go anywhere with him. She barely had energy to change into her nightshirt before falling into bed and into a deep sleep.

***

Horses thundered through Penny's dreams. In most of them she was the rider. A woman in a fashionable habit riding side saddle through a park alongside a river. A child, clinging with chubby hands to his saddle's pommel, as a man led his pony around a rink. A young man, encased in armor, riding a fiery war horse into battle.

The dreams came quickly, one after the other, ending with Penny being the horse itself, running free through hilly terrain, the smell of grass sweet in her nostrils. She pushed herself, muscles bunching, galloping up the incline, the earth firm beneath her hooves.

Other horses ran alongside her, all bare of saddles and bridles. Able to roam where they wished without the burden of a human sitting on their backs, pulling on the reins and telling them where to go. Absolute freedom.

She woke in a tangle of bed sheets, sweat cooling on her skin although the morning held a chill. She lay there a moment, recalling the joy of running free. As the euphoria faded, memories of the other dreams came tumbling back. The smell of straw and manure in the rink, the serene flow of the water in the river, and the stink of blood and fear as two armies came together, swords slashing.

The common thread, of course, was horses. She supposed the carousel ride from the day before conjured the dreams. Mixed with the stress of her injury, minor though it was, and the horror of watching the old man collapse right in front of her, it was enough to give anyone nightmares. Thank goodness Dora and Julie had been there.

She dragged herself off to the shower, still tired despite, or because of, the depth of sleep which had made it possible to dream so vividly. It was unusual for her dreams to be so intense. Usually she forgot about them soon after awakening. The horse dreams were as vivid as the dreams she'd had about Charlene and Victoria. Those dreams hadn't really been dreams, but memories, transferred into her sleeping mind, from the restless souls who had departed life, but not yet left the physical realm. However, these dreams were not about a person's life, but random snippets.

Dora was up, refreshing Plato's water bowl, when Penny came downstairs. She set the dish on the floor and poured dry food into its matching counterpart. Plato lapped up some water, but ignored the food for now, hoping to score some breakfast treats.

"He's awake," her sister said.

"Plato?" There was nothing unusual about that. Sometimes the dog awoke even before the girls, using the dog door they had installed for him to go out and do his business.

"No, silly. The carousel operator. The hospital just called. He's awake, coherent, and asking to see us."

"That's great. Maybe you and Julie can go visit him after your classes. He probably wants to thank you for saving his life."

"He wants to see you, too."

"Me? All I did was call 911."

"He asked for you specifically. He might want to thank you, but the hospital seems to think he's worried about your injury. Isn't that sweet? The poor man had a heart attack, but he still feels guilty about your little splinter."

Penny would not have described the splinter as "little." It had felt like Dora was digging a tree trunk out of her hand. However, it was nothing compared to a heart attack. "Check your schedule, talk to Julie and we will try to find a time that works for all of us."

"You're not closing tonight, right? I thought we could go after you get off work."

Penny agreed and the girls went their separate ways. She'd thought she might feel uncomfortable around Gage after their near date and her getting tipsy, but Gage didn't come in until late and then holed up in his office. She didn't even see him while on her lunch break.

Her hand was still tender to the touch, so she peeked under the bandage, but saw no signs of infection, just a red, swollen area. She babied it as much as she could, trying to do most of her carrying with her left hand. She hoped it wouldn't scar. The round, medallion-like burn scar in the center of her palm was weird enough.

She planned on rebandaging it when she got home, but by then it was feeling better and she forgot. Julie was already waiting at the house, and the three women piled into the little car Penny and Dora shared. The younger girls took the back seat, leaving Penny to feel like a chauffeur, or a soccer mom, as she drove them to the hospital.

They stopped at the hospital gift shop to buy a small plant. The hospital had given Dora the man's room number over the phone, so they skipped the front desk. The hospital had also told her the man's name was Elliot Jenkins.

Dora knocked on the door, which was ajar, and pushed it fully open. The old man sat propped up in bed, tubes stuck in his arms. The TV was on, with the volume turned down low.

"Come in," Elliot said, his voice hoarse.

"How are you feeling?" Dora asked. They trailed into the room, Penny hanging back. She didn't want to take the attention away from Dora and Julie.

"Like the horses stampeded over my chest."

"I'm sorry you're not feeling well," Julie said.

"That was a joke. I'm not doing too bad for an old guy with a bad ticker. Thanks to the two of you, I'm still here. You did an outstanding job."

"I was scared," Dora admitted. "We only practiced on a dummy."

"No one would ever know from your technique. The doctors think I have a few more years left in me. Time to mend fences with my son or find someone else to take over the carousel."

Penny found it strange, but endearing, that the man cared so much about a job which he must only work part-time and couldn't pay much more than minimum wage. She hoped the man reconnected with his son, but doubted the son would want to take on his father's job, especially if he had family and responsibilities of his own.

"I love this plant you gave me, but don't you think it looks thirsty? Why don't you find a nurse to give it some water while I talk to your sister?"

Penny glanced pointedly at the en suite bathroom, but the girls took the hint and wandered off. She stepped closer. "I'm really sorry about what happened. I shouldn't have made such a fuss about a splinter. I didn't mean to upset you."

"You didn't make a fuss. You were very gracious. More gracious than we deserved. You should hear some of those mothers when their little darlings get a scratch. Scary, but I guess it's the price we pay. Can I see?"

"There's not much to see. It's almost completely healed."

"Good. Just be sure it doesn't fester. Sometimes when she bites, she leaves a little something nasty behind."

Penny glanced out the door, hoping to see Dora and Julie on the way back. Should she just nod, as if the old man wasn't spouting nonsense? He actually seemed to think the wooden horse had bitten her. She thrust her hand towards him. "See, it's fine. Just a little splinter. No bite marks."

The old man took her hand in his. His hands were chilly and the skin papery thin. He gently traced the wound. "Still swollen, but it seems to be healing. Not like..." His voice trailed off, and he ran a finger over the raised scar of her burn.

Penny snatched her hand back. "That's from a previous injury."

The man's coffee-brown eyes held a hint of wonder. "You're marked."

"Just an old burn." Penny sighed with relief as Dora and Julie returned. "We'd better get going. Let Mr. Jenkins get some rest."

Dora set the plant on the windowsill where the man could see it, but it was out of the way. He thanked them all again.

"Come back if you get time. I'd appreciate the company." He spoke to them all, but his gaze met Penny's.

"Why did he want to talk to you in private?" Dora asked as they made their way back to the car.

"The hospital was right. He wanted to make sure I was okay."

"He should have been able to tell that just by looking at you."

"And he apologized. I think he's afraid I might try to sue or something."

Dora snorted. "A judge would throw that case right out the window."

Penny nodded. But she didn't really think Mr. Jenkins worried about a lawsuit. He appeared obsessed with the carousel, personifying it in his mind to where he thought the horse had actually bitten her. And what he had said about her being marked sent a shiver down her spine. She could lie to herself all she wanted about it being just a burn scar, but his words struck her as true. When she had touched that faulty wire on the Sunflower, something had changed. And she didn't think she would ever be the same again.

Chapter 4

The next few days passed in a flurry of ordinary activities. Work, school, caring for Plato and other chores. Penny's hand, while slow to heal, didn't get infected or leave a scar. Dora went to visit Mr. Jenkins again, but Penny made up an excuse. For all that the old man might suffer from dementia or confusion because of his heart condition, his dark eyes seemed too knowing for her peace of mind.

She closed Thursday night. Once everything was clean, she stopped by Gage's office to tell him she was leaving. As she leaned her head in the door, it reminded her of Sunday night when they'd shared a drink.

"I'm taking off." She stayed in the hall, afraid to cross the threshold. Did she want him to repeat the offer? Would she accept?

Gage looked up from counting the receipts. "Thanks, see you tomorrow."

"I'm off tomorrow."

"Right." Gage wrapped a rubber band around a stack of bills and slipped them in the cash bag. "Do you have plans?"

"Just the usual. Running errands, doing tarot readings, taking Plato for a walk, and relaxing with a book or TV show."

"I'm off tomorrow, too, if you'd like to do something. We could go out to lunch, let someone wait on you for a change."

Warmth spread through Penny's chest. "I'd like that."

"Great. I'll pick you up at noon. Be careful walking home." Gage buried himself back in his paperwork as if it was a page-turner and not an average day's take.

Penny hid a small smile. She'd never thought to see Gage flustered, but he seemed uncomfortable asking her out. His discomfort made her feel desirable and the walk home vanished beneath her ground-eating strides.

Dora was watching TV, Plato curled beside her on the couch. He wagged his tail when Penny entered, but didn't give up his comfy spot to greet her.

"Lazybones." She gave his head a scratch before plopping down in a chair. She pulled her shoes off. "My feet hurt."

"You seem rather chipper for just getting off work."

"That's because I have a date tomorrow."

"With Ben?"

Penny pulled a foot into her lap and began massaging it. "No, I told you we broke up."

"Yeah, but I don't understand why. He's such a nice guy."

"We're still friends. We just didn't work as a couple."

Dora dug a toe into the carpet. "Because you push everyone away."

"That's not fair. The break up was mutual."

"Really? He seemed to really like you. You must have put him off."

"It upset me when I nearly got electrocuted and blamed him for putting me in danger. I apologized later, since we were all at fault, but I guess it was too little, too late."

Dora was quiet for a moment as she considered Penny's explanation. "I would have thought he could forgive you anything, but guys can be unreasonable."

Penny knew her sister was thinking about her high school sweetheart, who blamed her for the accident that had ruined his life, even though he'd been driving and the other driver had probably been drunk. She changed feet and began working out the knots in her other foot.

"Well, who's the new guy? A customer at work?"

"Gage. We're going out to lunch."

"Your boss? He's old."

"To you, maybe."

"He must be in his thirties. And he's your boss. Haven't you heard about sexual harassment?"

"It's not like that. We've always been friends. Now we're just taking it a step further."

"First, he makes you assistant manager and then he asks you on a date. Sounds creepy to me."

Penny hadn't considered that her promotion might have anything to do with Gage's romantic interest in her. "You don't think I deserve the new position? Things have run smoothly since I took it on."

"I'm sure you're capable, but you haven't been there as long as some of the other employees. I just don't think you should go out with him. If it ends badly, you're going to be out of a job."

"Then I'll get another one." Penny stood, picked up her shoes, and turned towards the stairs. "I'm going to bed." She'd wanted her sister to be excited and happy for her, but Dora had made it seem like Gage was taking advantage of her. She knew it wasn't true, but now she couldn't get the idea out of her head that Gage had promoted her because he liked her rather than because of her abilities.

She dreamed, once more, of horses, wild horses racing through meadows and walking under towering trees. Since she didn't have to work, Penny slept in, but rose early enough to complete the tarot readings she had scheduled for the day. DrummerHyperbolic had come back for a few readings, and although he had not yet revealed his true identity, Penny believed he was the real deal. If she could establish a roster of celebrity clients, she wouldn't have to work at the cafe at all, removing any obstacles to her and Gage's relationship.

Unsure what to wear, she finally chose white Capri pants and a blue and white flowered blouse. It was cute, but casual. She brushed her copper-red hair until it shined and left it hanging loose. When Gage arrived, he wore jeans and a polo shirt. He often dressed informally for work, since he usually kept out of the public eye, so the collared shirt was a step up for him.

He suggested they go to one of the other restaurants within walking distance of Penny's house. Neither wanted to go to the cafe and eat under the eagle eyes of their coworkers.

It was another nice day, with just a slight nip in the air, so they ate outside. Penny relaxed as the waitress took their orders and brought over their drinks. The sun felt warm overhead, a handsome man sat across from her, and someone else was running her feet off fetching and carrying for them. A savory aroma in the air signaled her food would be delicious. The edginess she had felt since Mother's Day, when a man had nearly died right before her eyes and where she'd felt her role as Dora's unofficial guardian called into question, dissipated.

"I need to get out more often. Thanks for suggesting it."

"Any time."

Their sandwiches and fries came, and they dug in, sticking to innocuous topics of conversation such as the weather and minor gossip about other cafe employees. Gage mentioned they were going to lose one of their part-time servers in the fall when she went away to college.

"Too bad she's not staying local. Dora really likes her university."

"It's an excellent school, but most kids like to go away. Escape the influence of their parents."

Penny fiddled with her straw. Had she made a mistake by accompanying Dora to school? Did Dora need to get away from her? No, if Dora hadn't lost her hearing in the accident, Penny would have let her go alone, but as it was, Dora needed her.

"Do you have plans for the rest of the afternoon?" Gage asked.

"Not really."

"It's too nice a day to stay inside. Would you like to do something else?"

"Like what?"

"I don't know. Have you been to the zoo yet?"

"No."

"Then let's go."

Penny rarely acted spontaneously, preferring to plan her days. Years of not knowing where she would be the next day made her long for predictability. But suddenly she wanted to throw caution to the wind and just go with the flow. She agreed to Gage's suggestion, and they walked back to her house and picked up Gage's car.

"We won't be able to see everything in a few hours, but that gives us a reason to go back," Gage said.

Penny hugged the idea to herself as Gage drove out to Forest Park. The pleasant weather had drawn crowds, but they found a place to park on the street not too far from the entrance. A statue of sea lions greeted them, and Gage insisted on taking a selfie of them in front of it.

"What do you want to see first?"

"You're familiar with the place. Why don't you play tour guide?"

Penny had never seen Gage so relaxed. While he wasn't the type to yell, he set high expectations for his employees and himself. Losing his paranormal gift also weighed him down. He had confided in her about the government agency where he used to work, but had said little about his career-ending injury. Penny didn't know if the information was classified or if he just didn't want to talk about it.

Gage led her through the River's Edge, an area of the zoo starring the elephants. "You heard the saying 'an elephant never forgets?'"

Penny nodded.

"I don't know if that's true, but they are highly intelligent animals."

"Do you think they're happy, being locked up in a zoo?"

Gage shrugged. "Some of them were born here and have never known any other life. Conditions are a lot better now than they were years ago when they lived in cages. The zoo tries to give them as natural a habitat as possible."

A cage, even a gilded one, was still a cage, but at least the animals here were safe and well cared for. Who knows what might happen to them in the wild. Plato had been a stray when she and Dora took him in and she thought he was the happier for having regular meals, a comfortable home and lots of love.

After leaving the elephants, they passed by the Insectarium. Penny wasn't interested until she realized there was a walk-through butterfly exhibit, similar to the Butterfly House at Faust Park, but smaller.

"I can't look at the spiders. They make my skin crawl, but go ahead."

Gage smiled. "I think I can skip the spiders." They went straight to the butterfly area. Lush plant life and hundreds of colorful butterflies filled the enclosed space. To Penny's delight, one of them landed on her hand.

She stood still, trying not to scare the delicate creature. Gage snapped a photo, and it flew away.

"You only like the butterflies because they're pretty," Gage teased.

"Can the spiders help it if they're ugly?"

"Ugh. I could handle their ugliness if they weren't plotting to bite me."

"Speaking of biting, would you like a snack?"

They bought ice cream and ate it as they wandered past the bear pits. Penny paused in front of a large lake filled with flamingos and other birds. "Why do you think flamingos always stand on one leg?"

"I don't know."

They moved on. Hearing some music, Penny turned her head. Around the bend was a brightly painted carousel. She stopped as if she had run into a wall, fighting to breathe as pressure squeezed her lungs.

Gage nearly tripped over her. Looking to see what had caught her attention, he groaned. "Sorry, I forgot this was here. If it's giving you the creeps we can move on."

"No, it's just a carousel. It took me by surprise, that's all. It's not like if we rode it, the operator would have a heart attack. Right?"

"Of course not, but I understand if you'd rather not ride it, after what happened."

Penny gazed at the animals, recalling her vivid dreams of both riding horses and being a horse herself. This carousel was smaller than the one in the park. She assumed the zoo had commissioned it specifically. It wasn't just composed of horses. Riders could choose lions, tigers, and other animals.

"Maybe we should ride it. That's the common wisdom, isn't it? Get back on the horse after you fall off."

Gage's brows drew together. "You sound as though you actually are afraid to ride it. I have no desire to ride it—I get dizzy going around in a circle—but it's just a children's ride."

"I know, but there was something strange about the carousel at Faust Park. It seemed so well cared for, yet I got this giant splinter."

"I'm sure they take good care of it, but it is old."

"Houses can be haunted, so why not a carousel?"

"Whoa. Where is this coming from? Did you see a ghost?"

"No, but that's not my specialty."

A hint of frost entered Gage's blue eyes. "You've been having the dreams. Why didn't you tell me?"

"I don't know if they're 'dreams.'" She put the word in air quotes. "They might be nothing more than ordinary dreams. I have those, too."

Gage pulled her over to a bench. "Tell me."

Penny sat down next to him. "There's not much to tell. I've been riding lots of horses in my dreams, from ponies to massive war horses."

"That's it?"

"Sometimes I'm the horse."

"I know it shook you up when the operator had a heart attack. This sounds different from your telepathic dreams. I don't think you need to worry about them."

"They're definitely different than the dreams I had about Charlene and Victoria, but they're so colorful. Not like my normal dreams, which I usually forget five minutes after waking up."

Gage pressed his lips together as he considered her words. "You could ask Ben to go out there with you, but I think you're just scared. Maybe you should wait and see if these dreams go away."

Penny nodded. She didn't really want to contact Ben. The horse dreams had no coherent story, like when she had dreamed about the ghost from Sycamore House or the ghost haunting the Sunflower Showboat. She still felt responsible for Mr. Jenkins' illness, since he'd seemed to get so upset about her minor injury, but the man was old and might have been battling heart disease for years.

"Good. Then let's move on. The zoo will close soon."

"No, I think I should ride it. You don't have to come with me if it makes you sick. But I need to face my fears. And the money goes to a good cause." She pointed at the sign. Proceeds from the ride financed conservation efforts.

"Be my guest, but I'll sit it out."

Penny bought a ticket and got in line. She didn't have to wait long before getting on. The more unusual animals called to her, but she chose a horse. Once the music started and they spun around, she felt as if she had made a big deal about nothing. Even if the other carousel was haunted, it didn't mean that all carousels were dangerous. After all, she'd ridden on plenty as a child, and even the old rickety ones had been safe enough.

"Feel better?" Gage asked when she rejoined him.

"Much. No splinters, no dying employees. Fun."

"Great. We should have time to swing by the ape habitat before leaving."

They hurried through the ape exhibit and then walked back to the car. Tired, Penny was glad to leave the driving to Gage as he fought rush hour traffic.

"Do you want to come in?" Penny asked when they finally reached her house.

"Thanks, but I need to swing by the cafe. Keep the employees on their toes."

Relieved, Penny exited the car. She wasn't sure how Dora would react if she brought him in and didn't want to deal with the awkwardness of wondering whether he was going to kiss her. Because this had certainly felt like a date, even though they had only held hands.

Once again, he waited until she was safely inside before pulling away.

"Long lunch," Dora said from her position on the couch, a textbook in her hands.

"We went to the zoo afterward."

"How romantic."

"I had a good time. Rode the carousel." That got Dora's attention.

"It didn't weird you out?"

"It did, but I pushed through and nothing bad happened."

"You should go see Mr. Jenkins again. He asked after you when I went."

"Is he still in the hospital?"

"They were talking about transferring him to a nursing home, where he will stay until he's strong enough to take care of himself. So far they have been unable to reach his son."

Penny recalled he had mentioned a son to her. Perhaps she should visit him. He was probably lonely and once he was out of the hospital and no longer taking heavy doses of medication, he might not act so strangely. She'd faced part of her fears by riding another carousel. Maybe if she talked to the old man again, she would stop having the crazy dreams.

Chapter 5

*T*he carousel spun slowly before her, lights flickering. Music played, but instead of the cheerful tones she expected, the notes were sharp, soulful, and melancholic. Like the carousel at the zoo, this one was made of many animals. But like the historic carousel, her horse was there, the flying gold of her mane seeming to float in the breeze, her eyes watching and knowing.

Penny shivered. Children and a few adults rode the carousel, but their faces were blank and unmoving as if they were sleepwalkers.

Not wanting to challenge this carousel, Penny turned to go. However, she took only a few steps before a screeching sound caused her to look over her shoulder. To her dismay, the animals were pulling free of their poles. Wood cracked and metal wrenched, screws popping, as the carousel ground to a halt. Then, one by one, the animals leaped off the platform.

Some still had riders clinging to them, frozen as if they were the inanimate objects. On others, the riders slid off, crashing to the ground and shattering into dust. The wind picked up, whirling in a funnel, and sweeping the dust away.

"Leave me alone." She backed away as the animals moved closer, but they outnumbered her. Soon they surrounded her, blocking any chance of escape.

The golden horse, the one Penny had ridden at the park, drew close.

Get on.

The words sounded in Penny's mind as if the horse had put them there. The animal shook her head, tossing her mane, and the bells painted on her saddle chimed. Penny reached out and touched the horse's neck. Flesh, warm and damp with sweat, met her fingers. Grabbing on to the pommel, Penny placed her foot in the stirrup and pulled herself up on the saddle. The bells, now three dimensional, rang again.

The horse nickered, leading her motley crew of mismatched creatures across the field. Mist clung to the ground, making it difficult to see more than a few feet ahead, but the horse didn't require guidance. She led, taking Penny and the other animals where she wanted.

The music of the carousel, still mournful and out of tune, faded. They walked quietly, even their footfalls silenced by the thick carpet of greenery. No birds called. The meadow and surrounding woods appeared devoid of life.

They moved deeper into the trees, following a well-worn path. Penny wondered if she looked as still and solemn as the other riders, her skin a pasty gray. But when she looked down at her hands clutching the reins, they were still pink and healthy.

After what seemed like a long time, but might have been only minutes, Penny smelled smoke. They emerged from the woods into a small clearing ringed by towering trees. In the center of the clearing, a bonfire burned. It was huge. She could feel the heat from where she sat upon the golden horse. Flames shot towards the sky in a mixture of red and orange. It would have been spectacular at night, but it was still day, although a heavy covering of clouds blocked the sun.

The other riders slid to the ground and approached the bonfire, tossing sticks into its glowing center. Penny dismounted as well, but kept her distance from the fire, which threatened to burn out of control.

When their twigs burned away, the riders sat in a circle around the fire as if they were about to roast marshmallows or share campfire tales. Penny drew closer, but refused to join their ranks.

Begin.

Again the word sounded in Penny's head, but she didn't know what she should do. She soon realized the horse had not been speaking to her, but to the other carousel animals. They formed a circle around the riders, creaking as fur solidified back into wood. At last, only three animated animals remained. The golden horse, an antelope, and a lion.

The antelope made a high-pitched sound of fright, surprising Penny, who had not realized antelopes could vocalize. Then she took off, running into the woods. With a roar, the lion followed.

Something glued Penny to the scene, and she could still see the two animals long after they should have disappeared into the trees. The antelope made a valiant effort, but the outcome was set at the start. Inevitably she slowed as her heart could no longer pump fast enough or her lungs supply her with enough oxygen. The lion grew closer, tiring too, but with the scent of victory in his nostrils.

Penny tried to tear her gaze away, but she couldn't move, forced to watch as the lion leaped upon the antelope, claws tearing at the animal's sides, the wicked canines going for the throat, the powerful jaws ripping open the jugular.

Blood sprayed in a bright red arc, coating the verdant green foliage like an obscene Christmas display. The spell holding Penny still, shattered, and she looked away, stomach churning. It was part of nature. Lions had to eat, too. But the violence made her throat dry and her hands tremble.

I've got to get out of here.

Maybe no one would notice if she slipped down the path and back to the dismantled carousel. She took a few steps backward. No one paid any attention to her. The riders had risen from their place by the fire. Each now carried a knife.

Penny increased her pace. But they weren't looking at her. They gazed in the opposite direction, where the lion had gone. And to her amazement, the lion returned, dragging his kill behind him. He was going to share his meat with the riders as if they were all part of some strange tribe.

Unable to help herself, Penny broke into a run. She no longer cared how much noise she made, so long as she escaped from this bizarre scene. She felt the golden horse's gaze upon her, but heard nothing but her own labored breathing. Were they following her, their footsteps swallowed by the soft earth? Penny pushed harder.

She reached the meadow and tore across the flat ground. Her lungs burned as if they were on fire, air wheezing in and out. Discordant music echoed from the barren carousel, twirling endlessly around with empty poles. Penny staggered up to it, grabbed a pole as it came sailing by, and pulled herself onto the platform. She sank to her knees on the wooden floor and heard a bird cry overhead.

Penny awoke with a start, drawing air into oxygen-starved lungs. Her heart raced. She reached for her head, massaging her temples and calming her breathing. Was it just a dream or was her subconscious trying to tell her something?

Slipping into a comfy sweatshirt to ward off the morning chill, Penny knew where to go for answers. She walked to the hobby room and pulled out her tarot cards. Though she had used them for client readings, she hadn't read for herself since pulling the Wheel of Fortune card the day Dora had invited her to go on the Mother's Day picnic.

The invitation had touched Penny, but her life had been unsettled since then. Death had reached its cold, skeletal figure towards her when Mr. Jenkins nearly died from a heart attack. She was proud of

Dora for leaping into action and using her training to save a man's life. Sometimes she worried she wasn't doing enough for her sister, but Dora was doing well in school and appeared well grounded. Other times, she feared she might do too much. She didn't want to stifle her sister.

Her love life had changed as well. Gage had asked her on a date. Her insides went squishy as she recalled sharing an after-hours drink and walking hand in hand through the zoo. But then her budding relationship with her boss caused conflict with her sister. Up and down, the wheel spun.

Deciding to go for the classic past, present, future spread, she cut the deck and then laid out three cards. Page of Swords reversed, King of Cups and Page of Cups. Great. Three court cards, some of the most difficult cards in the deck to interpret.

Page of Swords in the past position. Pages represented youth and inexperience. She supposed she'd been inexperienced in the past, although she always felt older than her actual age. Swords were the suit of thought and ideas. Maybe her ideas needed honing. She had considered enrolling in college once Dora completed her degree. She didn't want to work as a waitress for the rest of her life.

The next two cards were both cups, the suit of emotion. The King of Cups, the master of emotions, was in the present position, followed by the Page of Cups, a beginner, in the future spot. That didn't seem to make sense.

She didn't feel as if she were the master of her emotions, like the King of Cups, so perhaps the card stood for a person in her life, and not an element of her own personality. An older man. Maybe Gage? While not as old as the middle-aged King, he was older than she was, which was part of the problem. Dora thought the age difference too big.

Where Gage was more settled, she was inexperienced. Not as young as the page, but certainly lacking polish. The only two serious relationships she'd been in had ended, the first badly, when her boyfriend had dumped her because she was spending too much time caring for her disabled sister. The second, Ben, had ended only recently. There had been no spark between them, even though Penny liked him and found him attractive.

The page held a cup, from which a fish poked his head and relayed a secret or message. Would the little fish give her the secret to making her relationship with Gage work?

Encouraged by the reading, but dissatisfied that it didn't appear to address her strange dreams, Penny put the cards away. She would consult them again later, when she'd formulated a specific question to ask.

In the meantime, she should contact Ben. She couldn't call him. It would be too awkward. Instead, she composed a text.

Penny: **How R U? Been having some weird dreams. Do you have time to get together?**

She read the message twice before pushing send because she didn't want to sound pushy or have him get the wrong idea. Her question wasn't a ruse to get them back together. She just wanted his professional opinion.

Ben: **Got some time before my next client arrives. Want to swing by the studio?**

Ben owned a photography studio relatively close to her house.

Penny: **Be there in a few.**

Ben: **Bring coffee.**

Penny smiled as she tucked her phone into her pocket. Maybe things wouldn't be that awkward after all.

She asked Dora to drop her off at Ben's studio on the way to school. If Ben couldn't give her a ride home, she would call a rideshare to get her home before work. She poured coffee into travel mugs, adding a shot of the same syrup they used at the cafe. It didn't make her home-made coffee as good as that at the restaurant, but it added something special.

"I'm glad you're going to see Ben. Maybe you can work things out." Dora was annoying cheerful for early morning and talked nonstop during the short drive to Ben's studio.

"I texted him, but we're not getting back together. I want to talk to him as a friend about some dreams I've been having."

"You're dreaming?" Dora took her attention off the road and the car drifted towards the center line. The driver of the car coming towards them lay on the horn and Dora jerked the steering wheel, guiding them back into their lane. "Since when? Why didn't you tell me?"

"At first I thought they were regular dreams. I'm still not sure it's anything to worry about."

"Where have you been lately where you might have picked up a ghost? The governor's house. Are you dreaming about him or his wife?"

"No. Just the carousel."

"You're dreaming about a carousel?"

"Horses mostly, but other carousel animals, too."

Dora pulled into the parking lot. "You're probably just upset be-cause of what happened to Mr. Jenkins."

"I'm sure you're right. But it will be good to talk to Ben anyway and clear the air." She got out of the car. "Have a good day at school."

Penny let herself in the back door and found Ben in his office, putting photos into portfolios. She handed him a coffee.

"You're a lifesaver. I'm trying to save money by not going to the coffee shop every day, but I ran out of the instant stuff here at the studio."

Penny took a sip of her own coffee and studied Ben. He looked the same as when they were dating. Still lanky, with brilliant blue eyes and a mop of unruly dark hair, he didn't appear to be suffering any ill effects from their break-up. She supposed she didn't either. Life went on, and she didn't think either of their hearts had been broken. Still, she felt a pang as she watched him struggle to slip the pictures into their plastic sleeves. He'd always been clumsy.

"Here. Let me do that."

Surprise crossed Ben's face, but he slid the portfolio over to her. He told her where to put each picture, and they finished the task in a few minutes.

"Tell me about the dreams."

Penny complied. "The first was a montage, like I was watching an old silent film. But last night was scary. It felt threatening."

Ben nodded. "I'll have to go see the carousel. See if I pick up any vibes. But these dreams are different from the others. I'm not sure you have anything to worry about... although the last one seems creepy."

"Thanks, I'd appreciate you checking it out."

"Have you talked to Juniper?"

"No, she's not at the library anymore and I'm sure she's busy with Adam."

"She still has access to the Internet and she can't be busy with the rock star every minute of the day. He must spend some time practicing."

"I'll call her." Penny sometimes wondered if the end of her relationship with Ben had more to do with Juniper finding Adam than her own failings. Although Ben had never tried getting back together with Juniper after a brief high school romance, she had nursed an unrequited affection for him for years. Or at least it had appeared to be unrequited. Penny was no longer so sure.

Ben glanced at his watch. "I'm glad you came to see me. I have just enough time to drop you back home before my first client of the day."

It felt familiar to slip into Ben's car, and she wondered if she should have tried harder. She'd wanted to take things slow, but maybe her caution had come across as disinterest. There might be some truth to Dora's accusation about her pushing people away.

Not wanting to delay Ben, she hopped out when they reached her house, but hesitated a moment before closing the door. "Come over for a reading sometime. On the house."

"I'll take it in exchange for checking out the carousel. You can come with me but I don't need you there if it makes you uneasy."

Unsure if Ben referred to her unpleasant experiences with the carousel or the discomfort which hovered between them, Penny forced a smile. She feared that returning to the carousel might enhance her dreams, but she didn't want Ben to think she was afraid of spending time with him.

"Let me know when you are going and I'll come along if it doesn't interfere with my work schedule." She waved Ben off and entered the house. Perhaps she should have mentioned she was now seeing someone else. It might have mitigated the tension.

Or it might have made it worse.

Chapter 6

Following up on her promise to Dora, Penny went to visit Mr. Jenkins the following morning. They had moved him from the hospital to a nearby nursing home.

The place was clean, and the staff appeared helpful. As nursing homes went, it wasn't bad, but Penny still hoped she could avoid spending time in such a place. Fortunately for Mr. Jenkins, he was only staying there until he regained his strength or his son arrived to take care of him.

"Good morning, Mr. Jenkins. Do you remember me? My sister helped save your life."

"Of course I remember you. Do you think I'm senile? Half the nurses in this place seem to think I am."

"I didn't mean to offend you. It's just that we didn't meet under the best circumstances. The hospital had you on a lot of drugs and..." Her voice trailed off.

"I said some strange things to you?" the old man asked, brown eyes twinkling.

"Yes, actually." Penny heaved a sigh of relief. It didn't seem as if Mr. Jenkins would suggest the horse bit her again.

"I didn't literally mean the horse bit you. I know she's made of wood. But she wants her due. Insists upon it."

Penny wished he hadn't referred to the horse as a female. In her dreams the horse was usually a mare, except for the war horse. And she did not know what he meant about "wanting her due." He still acted as though the carousel was alive. Maybe he was just that attached to it. "The carousel is a beautiful piece of workmanship and part of St. Louis history. You must be proud to take care of it."

Mr. Jenkins sat up straight. "I am. I've taken care of the carousel all my life. My father helped build it."

"Really?" Penny had heard about famous circus families, but hadn't known that kind of loyalty transitioned to amusement parks. Unless you were part of the owner's family.

"He was a master woodworker. Carved that horse from start to finish. He even selected which tree to fell."

Penny took note. Could Mr. Jenkins' father haunt the carousel? He seemed as deeply attached to it as the captain of the Sunflower Showboat.

"I'd hoped my son would take over the family business, but he ran away when he was a teenager. We haven't spoken since and the authorities haven't been able to find him." The sparkle in his eyes faded, and he picked at the sheet covering him. "I wasn't the best father. I was neglectful."

So was mine. A few weeks ago Penny had visited her dad in prison, intending to forgive him for dragging her and Dora around the country, bilking people out of their hard-earned money. Actually, she had already forgiven him in her heart, but had gone to tell him in person.

Her father hadn't been receptive. In his mind, he'd done nothing requiring forgiveness. And she believed he'd done the best he could. He'd never quite gotten over the shock and pain of his wife's desertion. He could have dumped them on his mother. Perhaps he should have. They would have had a more stable life. But for all his faults, he was warmer than Penny's grandmother, who had taken the girls in after her son landed in prison.

"Children can forgive a lot so long as there is love." Penny studied her hands clasped in her lap and avoided Mr. Jenkins' gaze. She didn't think this man, with his obvious devotion to the carousel, could have been too terrible a parent.

Mr. Jenkins reached over and squeezed her elbow. "You're very kind, my dear. I loved my son, but I didn't show it well. My work possessed me."

Penny knew of parents with prestigious jobs who ignored their children while building their careers, but she failed to see how operating a carnival ride could be so all-consuming. She didn't even think it would pay well enough to support a family.

"My father and the other woodworkers built the carousel for The Highlands, a popular amusement park that closed long before you were born. It ran every day, from morning until late at night. Thousands of people rode it." His eyes took on a dreamy look as he recalled a happier time. "My father sent me to care for it, getting me a job at the park. I never missed a day of work, save for the day Archie was born. Spent most of my waking hours there. Archie resented it."

"Kids always want more than their parents can give. What matters is that you did your best."

"I should have done better, but I can't change the past. All I can do is live in the present and look to the future." As he released her elbow, the sleeve of his hospital gown fell back, revealing a faded network of scars on his arm.

Penny stifled a gasp. If he were a younger man, she would have suspected him of cutting himself. Although she wasn't an expert, she thought cutting disorder only affected young people. Perhaps the scars were old. She was so absorbed in her own thoughts, she nearly missed what he said next.

"I want you to take over the carousel for me. She likes you. And with my son gone..."

"I already have a job."

"A job, yes, but do you have a career? You could run it temporarily while I recover, but I want you to consider making the carousel your life's work, as I've made it mine."

"I'm flattered by your trust in me, but I have no interest in working for the park service." She doubted it paid as much as her current job.

The man waved away her excuse. "Sure, the park service signs your paycheck, but it's not your real employer. Think of how happy you will make all the children who ride it."

"Sure, kids are great, but I'm not that good with them. And I don't think the job would pay enough to support me and my sister."

"It's a great deal of responsibility and the pay reflects that."

"Thanks for the offer, but I need to keep the job I have. It's within walking distance from my house which allows Dora to take the car to school."

"Just think about it."

"I will," Penny said to appease him, although she had no intention of doing so.

Mr. Jenkins leaned back against the pillows. "Would you pour me a glass of water?"

"Of course." She reached for the pitcher and cup on his tray. "Then I need to go. I have to get to work." And Mr. Jenkins was looking drawn and tired.

"Think about it," he reminded her as she left the room.

Penny waved back at him. Although she still didn't intend to consider the job, lately her life seemed to revolve around carousels.

***

A couple days after she visited Mr. Jenkins in the nursing home, Penny received a text from Ben telling her he intended to go check out the carousel that afternoon. Penny switched shifts with another server, who was closing, so she could accompany him.

He picked her up after lunch and they drove out to Faust Park. The park wasn't as crowded as it had been on Mother's Day, so they parked in the inner lot.

"How is this going to work?" Penny asked as they walked to the building housing the carousel. Usually Ben performed his seances at night and out of sight of the public.

"I'm not doing a seance. I think people might get concerned if I light candles and try to talk to dead people."

Ben held the door open for her, but ruined this suave move by tripping over the threshold. He muttered something under his breath.

"Careful, people get hurt around here."

"I don't think I'm going to have a heart attack."

"Watch out for splinters."

Ben gave her a confused look and Penny realized she hadn't mentioned her splinter to him. "I'm just being silly. The operator, Mr. Jenkins, got upset because I got a splinter and I think he thought I might try to sue. The distress might have precipitated his heart attack."

Ben frowned. "You didn't tell me about the splinter. Did it bleed?"

"Oh, yeah. It was wicked, although Dora says I was a baby about it."

He didn't crack a grin or tease her. "Can I see?"

"Nothing to see now." Penny held out her hand.

Ben took it, his thumb circling the scar on her palm.

"No scar this time."

"Right. It's probably nothing. Have you had any more electrical events?"

Ben was referring to the shock she had received on the Sunflower, which had initially burned her. Another jolt, from the same power outlet, helped her disable his kidnapper. "No. I think the electrician made a mistake when he wired the Sunflower. Something is wrong with that switch." She decided not to mention that streetlights seemed to flicker more often now. That might be nothing more than her imagination.

Ben released her hand. "I'm just going to get a feel for the place. I'll walk around, see if I feel any cold spots."

They meandered around the ride, which was only half full. Penny glanced at the middle-aged woman running it. The park service had already replaced Mr. Jenkins, even if she was only a temp. He probably didn't have any authority to offer her the position. Not that she was interested in taking it, anyway.

"I'm not picking up anything, but ghosts are more active at night. I'm going to ride. Should I get you a ticket?"

Penny shook her head. After her latest dream, the thought of getting on one of the carousel animals made her nauseous. "I'll watch. But ride the golden horse if she's free. Just be careful. She must have a rough spot where I picked up that splinter."

Ben got on the next rotation and chose the golden horse. Penny watched from the sideline. The horse was a beautiful work of art, but not as lifelike as she remembered. Perhaps her memories were blending with her dreams.

The few minutes Ben was on the ride seemed to take forever. Finally, the music stopped, and the ride wound to a stop. She was waiting at the exit when he came out.

"What did you feel? Tell me everything."

Ben guided her out of the way so other people could exit. "I'm sorry, but I felt nothing out of the ordinary."

Penny's shoulders slumped. "I was so sure it was the carousel causing the dreams, but we also toured the governor's house. We could go there, but it's only open certain weekends."

"If your dreams center on the carousel, I don't think the governor's house is relevant. They might be regular dreams. If you're really concerned, I saw on the website that you can rent this place out for parties. Probably can't rent it at midnight, but at least it would be dark."

"Sounds expensive." However, if she was working there, she might be able to sneak Ben inside. Penny pushed the thought from her head. She couldn't work there even if she wanted to. They had already hired someone else for the job. Besides, she had just gotten a promotion at her current job. It would be unprofessional to leave Gage in the lurch.

"Probably not worth it," Ben agreed. "I think I would feel something, even during the day, if there was an active haunting."

"Well, thanks for checking."

"No problem. Can I stop by tomorrow for my tarot reading?"

They arranged a time for him to come over, and Ben drove her back home. She had to get ready for work, so there wasn't an awkward pause while she decided whether to invite him in. She was hopeful they could put the past behind them and move forward as friends.

But she still felt a pang as she watched him drive away.

Chapter 7

Archie Jenkins tossed his cigarette in the grass and ground it out with his foot. It irritated him that according to new employee rules he had to exit the theme park just for a quick smoke. It had been much easier when there were designated smoking areas in the park. Easier for customers, too. Seemed like management not only wanted to grind down employees but also lose out on sales. The way things were going, all the workers who smoked would end up quitting. And then who would run their stupid rides?

Archie didn't like theme parks and didn't understand why people wanted to spend their hard-earned money standing in line all day and eating overpriced and under-tasty food. The joy that some fools took from riding a roller coaster or getting soaking wet on a water ride made him sick. It reminded him of his dad and the old man's obsession with his fancy carousel. You would have thought he was actually doing something important from the pride he took in running what was little more than a glorified merry-go-round.

He chugged on his water bottle, washing the taste of smoke from his mouth. Time to head back. If he was late one more time, his supervisor might fire him. As if he cared. There was always another job at another park somewhere. Archie had lost track of the number of theme parks he'd worked at. He'd even worked at Disney for a few months, before being let go for "attitude problems", whatever that meant. Actually, it had bummed him out to lose that job. He hated how fake it all was, but took a certain satisfaction from working at the number one theme park in the world while his old man still puttered around dusting off that old carousel at a city park. The old ride had survived the fire which had destroyed The Highlands, but then had been turned into nothing more than playground equipment.

He'd gotten an email from a hospital in St. Louis a few days ago. His dad was on his deathbed and wanted to see his long-lost son one more time. Archie didn't buy it. As far as he knew, the old man had never looked for him before. Why bother now?

It had been easier to disappear in those days. Back then, there were no computers or cameras tracking your every move. At first, being young and with limited experience, he'd worked at small-time carnivals, many of which had paid him under the table. It was only later than he'd dug out his social security number and taken jobs at the bigger theme parks.

He didn't think he'd go home. What was the point? His dad had put his work for The Highlands above his family, had cared more about a stupid hunk of wood more than his own son. His only reason for returning to St. Louis would be if he was going to inherit something, which, considering where his dad had worked, wasn't likely.

He returned to the pirate ship ride where he was stationed and exchanged places with the employee who had spelled him for his break.

"You're late. Again." The kid was still in high school, young enough to be Archie's son, not that Archie had ever wanted a family.

"What of it. I was running rides while you were still in diapers."

The kid shrugged. "The supervisor is going to write you up. Again."

"Get going and mind your own business." Archie hated the newbies who thought they were so much better than the old-timers. Sometimes he wondered why he continued to work in theme parks, but it was all he knew.

His supervisor caught up with him when he went on his lunch break. "Archie, I've told you we can't tolerate tardiness. We run a tight ship here. When you're late, it pushes everyone else behind schedule."

Who cares? "Won't happen again."

"You said that last time."

"I'm worried about my dad. He's sick."

The supervisor looked taken aback. Archie rarely talked about his personal life. "I'm sorry to hear that. I was going to fire you, but let's go with a suspension. You go see your father, clear your head and come back ready to work. Take two weeks without pay."

Archie's eyes narrowed. "One will do."

"Take the offer. You're not getting a better one."

"Fine." Archie turned and walked away.

"Starting now," the supervisor called after him.

Archie waved him off and headed for the park exit. Guess the old man was going to get that visit after all.

***

When Penny got home from work, she curled up on the couch with a glass of wine and checked her email. Dora had gone to a frat party with some friends, so she wouldn't be home until late. Plato hopped up beside her and she pet him with one hand as she scrolled through messages. Among the junk and a few items of interest, two messages stood out.

The drummer from Hyperbolic was so pleased with the readings she had done so far that he wanted to do an in person reading and would pay for her travel expenses. Of course, she still wasn't sure he actually was the famous drummer. She needed to find out before committing. But having a high-profile client would do wonders for her tarot business. She sent a quick text to Juniper, asking if she had met Hyperbolic's drummer.

The second came from the county park department. Upon recommendation of their long-time employee, Elliot Jenkins, they wanted to offer her the position of caretaker and ticket collector for the historical carousel at Faust Park. Penny set her phone on the table and sipped her wine. Apparently Mr. Jenkins had pull with the park department.

She clicked on the link within the email to view the details. The job was temporary, lasting only until Mr. Jenkins returned to work. But if they were happy with her performance during the trial period, she would be eligible for permanent hire when Mr. Jenkins retired. The offer hinted at the possibility of finding her another position within the park service after her temporary job ended, but before Mr. Jenkins' retirement.

Even more surprising than the park service offering to hire her just on Mr. Jenkins' recommendation was the terms of employment. Although she would work fewer hours than she now worked at the cafe, she would make almost as much money. The job description explained that she would be in charge of maintaining the carousel, selling tickets, and running the ride. This involved cleaning, performing routine maintenance, and working with art historians, if necessary, to keep the valuable piece of St. Louis history in top working order.

The offer tempted her. The job would free up time she could devote to growing her tarot business. And it would allow the burgeoning romance between her and Gage to proceed without the awkwardness which came from him being her boss.

However, she continued to dream about horses and carousels, although none of her recent dreams had been as disturbing as the dream with lion and antelope. Despite Ben not seeing any ghosts, Penny felt sure something was there. If not a ghost, then what? The energy didn't seem to match the unknown entity she had sensed on the Sunflower. She rubbed the scar on her palm. When questioned, she blamed faulty wiring for her own accident and her ability to incapacitate the casino manager. And she thought there was something wrong with that light switch. But there was more to it. Someone, or something, had chosen her. As Mr. Jenkins had noticed, she'd been marked.

Marked for what, she did not know.

Penny's phone dinged as a text came in from Juniper.

Juniper: **Jackson is a great guy. He is impressed with the readings you've done for him.**

Penny: **Thanks. I wasn't sure it was really him. Did Adam recommend me?**

Juniper: **I did. He was moping around and needed guidance.**

Penny: **Thanks so much. I may come out to give him an in-person reading. Maybe I'll see you?**

Juniper: **Maybe. It would be nice to catch up.**

Excited, but even more nervous now that she knew her client was actually a famous drummer, Penny took a deep breath and turned her attention to the email from the park service. She expressed her interest in the job and agreed to meet with human resources. She would take it one step at a time. Perhaps Gage would allow her to take a leave of absence from the cafe. If not, and the park couldn't find a place for her, she could always get another waitressing job.

Transportation would be a problem, but she'd been saving money from her tarot readings. She could afford an old clunker.

She didn't expect a response until the next day since it was outside of business hours, but almost immediately another email popped into her inbox. Human resources would call the next day to arrange an interview.

Penny turned her attention to the email from the drummer. If she was going to do an in-person reading for him, she'd better schedule it quickly, since she might soon have a new job.

***

Juniper heaved a sigh of relief as Adam dropped a quick kiss on the top of her head and went to join his fellow band members on stage for a practice session. While it was exciting to tour with a band, she was an introvert and found the tight quarters draining. Fortunately Adam, being introverted himself, understood and tried to make sure she got some time to herself. They would practice for at least an hour, maybe longer, and she would be blissfully alone.

When her phone buzzed with an incoming call, she almost didn't answer it. How dare someone disturb her precious quiet time? However, when she saw it was Penny calling, she pushed the accept button. Ben never called, although he responded to her texts. Penny might have news of him.

"Hello?"

"Hey, I'm glad I reached you. I know you must be busy, but do you have a few minutes to talk about a potential case with me?"

Juniper hesitated, tempted to ask Penny to call back. But if she was working on a case, that meant she was in contact with Ben. "What's up?" She listened as Penny told her about riding a carousel, getting a splinter, the operator's heart attack, and her own strange dreams.

"What does Ben think?"

"That's the problem. He went out to the site and felt nothing. But it was during the day and lots of people were around."

Juniper chewed on a fingernail, realized what she was doing, and forced herself to stop. She would never develop the long, polished nails of the other girlfriends in the band if she couldn't stop nail-biting. "Do you want me to research the carousel?"

"That would be great. We already know a few things about it. It's a beautiful old piece originally built for The Highlands amusement park. Mr. Jenkins, the operator, has worked on it his entire career."

"I'll see what I can discover." She twirled the ends of her midnight black hair around her finger. "How is Ben? I don't hear much from him. I think he's still angry with me for acting so impulsively."

There was a long pause before Penny spoke. "Fine. His business is doing well."

"I would expect nothing less. He's an excellent photographer." The urge to chomp on her fingernail was overwhelming, but she resisted. "Does he ever mention me?"

"I know you've been out of the loop, but I thought someone would have told you. Ben and I are no longer dating. I haven't seen much of him either."

Butterflies churned in Juniper's stomach. Ben was no longer seeing Penny? Was he single or seeing someone else? And what difference did it make? She had made her choice and was with Adam now. "I'm sorry. I didn't know."

"Are you sorry?" Penny's voice was sharp. "I always got the feeling you wanted Ben for yourself."

It was nothing more than the truth. Juniper didn't know why she felt so defensive. "Don't blame me for your break-up. I had nothing to do with it. I admit to crushing on Ben, but that's before I met Adam."

"True, a regular guy can't compete with a rock star."

"What are you saying?"

There was another silence, followed by a deep sigh. "I'm sorry. You're right. Our break-up wasn't your fault, although I think it played a part. Losing you sent Ben into a tailspin. I was collateral damage."

"Ben had years to ask me out. He never did. Does he only want me because someone else has me?" She gave up the battle and nibbled on the edge of her index finger.

"Does someone else have you? If you want Ben, he's ripe for the taking."

Juniper wished she hadn't taken the phone call. Her nerves jangled, and she could give up on relaxing during her break. "I've got to go. I'll let you know what I find out about the carousel."

She ended the call and paced around the green room. They were in a mid-sized city, she'd forgotten which one, and the room was nicer than the smoky, cramped room found in small venues. There were several couches to sit on, as well as tables to gather around. She took her laptop out of its carrying case and settled on the most comfortable looking sofa. As she waited for the computer to boot, she considered what Penny had shared.

Ben was single. He missed her. He'd even broken up with Penny, in part because of her. Not for a minute did she think it was the only reason. There had to have already been cracks in their relationship. But her unexpected and uncharacteristic actions had driven a wedge into those cracks.

She could return home to the safety and familiarity of the library. She could go back to the man she had loved since they were teenagers and experience, for real, the fantasy she'd concocted in her mind.

But to do so, she would have to give up Adam. Her ribs seemed to contract around her heart, squeezing it painfully. She couldn't sacrifice her relationship with Adam. She loved him.

Or did she love the lifestyle, the fame, and the money? No, she hated being crammed into a tour bus with so many other people. The lack of privacy wore her down. And she hadn't forgotten how horribly the press had treated her when they found out she was dating Adam while he still had an official girlfriend. She'd almost lost her job and hadn't been able to leave the house without being harassed.

She had to admit the money was nice, but she loved Adam despite his lifestyle, not because of it. She needed to leave Ben where he belonged—in the past.

Comforted by her thought process, Juniper set her turbulent emotions aside and pulled up a couple of specialized databases. She was on leave from the library, so still had access to their resources, along with a few she subscribed to on her own. She also did a basic browser search.

She soon confirmed the information Penny had already given her. The carousel had been an elaborate and expensive purchase for The Highlands amusement park. But its beauty made it popular with both children and adults, so the owners of the park probably made good on the investment.

A fire, which investigators believed had started in a cooking area, had destroyed most of The Highlands. Fortunately, the carousel survived. A local business owner purchased it and later donated it to the county. It had operated for years at another park before being restored and moved to its current location.

She then went deeper and found what she was looking for—a reference to the carousel being haunted. According to the account she read, a pair of children haunted the ride. There was no mention of the carousel animals coming to life.

She dug some more, but found nothing else. Was there any truth to the story of the ghostly children? And did they have anything to do with Penny's dreams? In the other two cases Juniper had helped them solve, Penny had experienced dreams from the point of view of the ghost, uncovering bits of their lives and the tragic deaths that had led to their hauntings. Things seemed different here. Was it because the ghosts were children and had only a brief life prior to death? Or was something else going on, something unconnected with the child ghosts, if they even existed. Ben had not sensed their presence.

Juniper closed her laptop and pushed it aside. She only had a few minutes before Adam and the boys would return, and she intended to spend them inside the pages of a book.

Chapter 8

Penny's interview with the park department went so well they offered her the job on the spot. She agreed to start next Tuesday, although she felt bad about leaving the cafe without notice. She hoped Gage would understand.

Since she was already in the neighborhood, she stopped by the nursing home and thanked Mr. Jenkins for getting her the job.

"He already has a visitor, but go on up," the receptionist told her. Hoping Dora had found time to visit, Penny took the elevator to Mr. Jenkins' floor and hurried to his room. A middle-aged man with broad shoulders, thinning hair, and a bit of a paunch stood by Mr. Jenkins' bed. Penny stopped in the doorway.

"Good morning, Mr. Jenkins. Am I interrupting? I can come back later." She wondered if the man was Mr. Jenkins' son.

"Not at all. Come in. This is my son, Archie."

Penny stepped inside the room and held out her hand. "Penny Sparks."

"This is the young lady I was telling you about. Her sister saved my life."

"Guess I owe your sister some thanks. Dad and I lost touch over the years."

"She was happy to help. She's studying physical therapy and planning to make a career out of helping others."

"Kind of like what we do, son. Archie followed in my footsteps and has worked at many theme parks over the years."

Penny wasn't sure what theme parks had to do with the health care industry, but nodded politely.

"We help people," Mr. Jenkins explained. "Thousands of people flock to theme parks every year for a chance to relax, have fun, and spend time with their families."

"It's not that great a job. Nothing like being a doctor," Archie said.

"Penny might disagree. She's considering running the carousel until I get better."

Archie looked up at that, his dark, flat gaze meeting hers. Although his eyes were brown, like his father's, they held none of the older man's warmth. "Is that right? You always told me I'd be in charge of the carousel when you retired."

"I didn't know where to find you. And I didn't think you wanted the job. You told me often enough when you were a boy that you hated the carousel."

"I don't want the job, but you should have asked before giving it to someone else."

Mr. Jenkins seemed to deflate against his pillows. "I guess I should have given it more time."

Penny, who hadn't been sure when she left for her interview this morning, if she really wanted the job, suddenly had no intention of giving it up. But she didn't want to get involved in family squabbles. "I'd better get going. Nice to meet you, Archie."

"Wait, let's grab a cup of coffee in the lounge. Get to know each other a bit. Like I said earlier, I owe you and your sister for taking care of my dad when I wasn't able to."

Penny had no desire to go anywhere with this man, but the older Mr. Jenkins was looking at her with a hopeful expression on his face. "I could use a quick cup of coffee, but I don't have a lot of time."

Archie smiled at her in a way that reminded her of a shark and gestured for her to leave the room first. Penny did, conscious of him at her back. Down in the lounge, they poured cups of coffee and sat in adjacent chairs.

The smile fell from Archie's face as he dropped all pretense. "Game's up. If you thought you could sucker some old man into leaving you his assets, think again."

Penny sat up straight, pressing her spine against the back of the chair. "I'm not trying to trick your father or take anything from him. My sister saved his life. We came to visit because she wanted to make sure he was okay."

"But then you kept coming."

"He's a kind old man. And he had no one else to visit him." But Penny admitted to herself that her behavior was odd. She wasn't exactly the type to make a habit of visiting the sick. She wasn't trying to worm her way into his will, but he was her primary connection to the carousel, which continued to haunt her dreams.

"I'm here now. And it's more than the old man should expect after years of neglect."

"Now that I know he has family watching over him, I don't need to return." She'd call to check on his father's progress, however, since she didn't trust Archie to see to his best interests. She set her mostly untouched cup of coffee on the table.

"He got you the job after you almost got him killed."

"What? He had a heart attack."

"A heart attack brought on by the stress caused by you trying to turn a minor injury into a big deal."

Penny's cheeks heated as she stood. "I've had enough of your abuse. I told your father I was fine, but he worried. It wasn't my fault."

"You want the job."

"It's just a part-time, temporary position." Should she offer it to him? He seemed keen to have it, but she didn't want to give it up. And she knew she would take better care of the valuable landmark.

"Don't you forget it. Once my dad's back on his feet, you'll be out on the street. I guarantee it. And when he kicks it for good, the job will be mine. He's been telling me that since I was a small boy."

There was such venom in Archie's face that Penny nearly told him he could have the job, pending park service approval. But when she opened her mouth, the words wouldn't come. Instead, she hurried out of the room, feeling his eyes on her back the whole time. She could hardly believe the nice old man who'd been so concerned about her splinter had such a nasty son.

But although she could scarcely credit anything that came out of that man's mouth, his accusations had hit a little too close to home. She wasn't after Mr. Jenkins' assets, which she guessed were minimal. And she hadn't been looking for a job. But she had been after something, perhaps the old man's approval. She hadn't consciously sought to ingratiate herself with him, but then she didn't think her father deliberately set out to con people either. He always thought that this time he would deliver, this time he would provide value. It was part of what made him such a great sales agent. And it was a skill she wanted nothing to do with. If she had somehow conned Mr. Jenkins into giving her the job, it made her feel sick.

But she couldn't deny the job offer was tempting.

***

The altercation with Archie put Penny behind schedule. She hurried home and got ready for her shift. She greeted Susan as she entered the cafe and only had time for a quick cup of coffee before she started taking orders. Business was steady, but not frantic, and her tips added up. That was one thing she was going to miss when she stopped waiting tables. Still, she thought she would make more money overall if she could take on a few more tarot clients.

She wanted to talk to Gage, so she didn't rush through cleaning and set up once the cafe closed. When Susan left, she went to his office.

Gage greeted her with a smile, and her breath hitched. He didn't smile often, but when he did, it made him look younger. His blue eyes were soft, like the sky on a cloudy day. "Did everything go all right in the dining room? Sorry I didn't get out there at all tonight. I was following a promising line of research."

"Really?"

"Ron's magical wards at the casino impressed me, so I've been looking into the possibility of magic restoring my viewing ability."

Penny wrinkled her nose. After her unintentional, but possible, use of magic the day she'd cooked at the cafe, she'd distrusted it. At first, she hadn't even believed Gage's theory that she had put a spell on the soup, turning the lunch patrons into brawlers. Despite clear evidence of ghosts, she wasn't sure she believed in magic. After hearing from Ben how Ron had trapped him in the hotel room with some kind of binding spell, she was open to the idea, but still didn't see how she could have any powers when she'd never studied the craft.

"Some people study magic, but others inherit innate ability," Gage had explained to her.

"Any luck?"

"Not yet."

"I wanted to let you know I'm going to need some time off from the cafe. The carousel operator suggested I fill in for him while he's recuperating and the park department offered me the job. I start on Tuesday."

Gage's brows drew together. "Do you think that's a good idea? Are you still having the dreams?"

"Yes. Ben sensed nothing out of place when we went out there, but I think things will become clear if I'm with the carousel every day."

"And you didn't think to discuss this with me? I made you assistant manager so I wouldn't have to deal with staffing crises."

"You're the owner. You can't escape personnel problems." But she felt guilty.

"I suppose you expect your job to be here waiting for you when you come back?"

Anger overrode Penny's guilt. "I'll handle the schedule so you won't have to dirty your hands with it. If I bump up the hours of our part-time staff, we can get by for a few weeks without hiring extra help. The carousel is closed on Mondays. I can come in then if you really need me."

Gage drummed his fingers on his desk. "You seem to have thought this out."

"I'm sorry I didn't give you more notice, but the park service offered me the job this morning and I wasn't about to turn it down."

"I don't understand. It's a temporary, part-time job. I know you don't make that much money here, but now that you're fulltime you get benefits and the promotion came with a raise."

"I'm grateful and want to keep the job, but if you feel you can't hold it for me, I understand. It's a risk I'm willing to take."

"Why?"

"Why is everyone standing in my way? Mr. Jenkins' son is all bent out of shape because he expected the job would go to him and now you're trying to take this opportunity away from me."

"I'm not trying to take anything away from you, but I'm not sure you're thinking clearly. When we went to the zoo last week, you didn't even want to ride the carousel. The entire experience freaked you out. Now you think nothing of inconveniencing me and throwing away a decent job so you can spend your days dealing with overexcited children. Something doesn't add up."

"I'm sorry for the inconvenience, but this isn't about you. I don't want to be a server all my life."

Gage dropped his gaze to his cluttered desk. "Understandable. You're bright and capable. That's why I promoted you."

"I didn't mean it like that. I just don't want to still be doing the same thing twenty years from now."

Gage shuffled his stack of papers. "Don't let me keep you from bigger horizons. No need to stick around here. I'll manage the schedule."

Things were not going the way Penny had envisioned. She'd expected Gage to be happy for her, even though she knew it would make things more difficult for him. Maybe she had misinterpreted the drink, their lunch date, and the trip to the zoo. Now, not only was she unsure if they were dating, she didn't know if she still had a job. "I'd better get going before Dora worries about me. See you tomorrow?"

"Sure." Gage didn't look up from his desk.

Penny heaved a sigh and headed for the exit. At least he hadn't fired her... yet.

Chapter 9

The next few days were tough. Gage was cool at work. He'd called her into his office and gone over a plan with her. If she could schedule the other employees around her absence, he would hold her job for two weeks. If Mr. Jenkins wasn't able to come back to work by then, they would renegotiate. He didn't ask her out again or offer to share his alcohol stash. The other employees gave her a wide berth as if she had some contagious disease.

Dora also complained about the new job. She wasn't happy about having to get a ride to school until Penny found another car they could afford. On Tuesday morning, Penny beat her downstairs, even though Dora had to leave earlier. She fed Plato and fried up a pan of scrambled eggs before her sister entered the kitchen, rubbing sleep from her eyes.

"I should never have forced you to come along when I went to visit Mr. Jenkins. Now you seem as obsessed with that stupid carousel as he is."

"Don't be ridiculous. I haven't spent my life tending to it. It's an important piece of history."

"Since when did you become interested in history?"

"Since forever. Why do you think I rented this house?"

"I still think it's a dumb move. You pissed Gage off, just another example of your lousy track record with men."

"He'll get over it." Penny hoped it was true. If not, there were more important things in life than men. "Have some eggs."

Dora heaped some eggs on her plate and grabbed a soda out of the fridge. "Sorry. My track record is as bad as yours. At least you're out there trying."

"Maybe it's time you put Win behind you. Have you met any cute boys at school?"

"Sure, but I'm concentrating on my studies for now."

Penny shot a sideways glance at her sister. It might be the truth. Dora was smart, but even with her hearing aid she had to work harder than others to keep up. But Penny worried her sister might still be in love with her ex. "Good for you. And I'm concentrating on my career."

"No, you're not. You're putting the best job you've ever had at risk to play with a carousel."

"I didn't tell Gage, since he was already mad at me, but if I do a good job, there's a chance I can have the job permanently once Mr. Jenkins retires."

"So? It's not even full-time hours. If you want to change jobs, start taking classes at the university."

"With more free time I can grow my tarot business."

"That makes sense. Why didn't you say so in the first place?" Dora had pressured Penny to read tarot cards again after a long hiatus.

"I expected you, and Gage, to support me in my decisions without having to justify them."

"You're an adult. You can do as you please. But why wouldn't your friends let you know if they thought you were making a mistake? And Gage was counting on you."

A worm of guilt wriggled through Penny's mind. She had let Gage down. The cafe should run smoothly for the next couple weeks if no one got sick, but her absence stretched the staff thin. "Can I count on you to take a shift or two if necessary?"

Dora's mouth gaped open until she remembered she was eating and snapped it shut. "I've never worked as a server before."

"I know, but you've eaten at plenty of restaurants and you've watched me. You could handle it."

Dora swallowed her bite of eggs. "Only if it's a genuine emergency. And you have to pay me."

"Deal. Get ready. I'll run you over to school, but you'll have to find a ride home."

When Dora left to get dressed, Penny washed the dishes. Plato gazed at her longingly. She patted him on the head. "I'll take you for a quick walk after I drive Dora to school."

The girls piled into the car. When Penny turned the key, the engine made a clunking sound, but didn't turn over. Several more tries produced the same result. Penny banged her head against the steering wheel. "The battery must be dead."

"Maybe we can get a jump."

"From who?" The girls weren't well acquainted with their neighbors, and most had probably already left for work.

"Call Ben... or Gage."

"Not Gage. He's already mad at me." She pulled out her phone and rang Ben. When she explained their predicament, he offered them the use of his car.

"But you'll have to come get it. I'm tied up with appointments."

Dora didn't react well to the news. "I don't have time to walk all the way over to Ben's studio. I'll be late." She pulled out her own phone and called Julie.

With Dora taken care of, Penny hitched Plato up to his leash. It was a long walk, but she had plenty of time. Ben was busy with customers when she arrived, but excused himself to hand her the keys.

"Thanks, Ben. It would be awful to be late on my first day."

A shadow passed over Ben's face. "Are you sure this is a good idea? I sensed nothing unusual, but since you've been having dreams, I think you should keep your distance from the carousel."

Penny closed her hands tightly over the keys, afraid Ben might try to snatch them back. "Not you, too. Archie Jenkins thinks I stole his inheritance, Gage is mad at me for leaving him in the lurch, and Dora thinks..." Penny remembered who she was talking to. "Well, it doesn't matter what she thinks. I hoped you would be on my side."

Ben raised his hands in surrender. "I am on your side. But usually you're the one trying to talk me out of investigating. We seem to have switched positions."

"Exactly why I thought you would support me."

Ben shook his head. "I've got to get back to my clients. Don't wreck my car."

Plato wiggled with joy at the bonus of a car ride after his long walk. Penny dropped him at the house before driving to the park.

She used her key card to open the building and flipped on the lights. She flinched when the switch gave her an electric shock, then chided herself for stupidity. Everyone got a shock now and then.

She walked around the carousel, checking out the animals. She took special care with the golden mare, running her hands over the painted wood, but not finding any rough areas that she thought might give an unsuspecting rider a splinter. Noticing a spot of blood on the horse's curved neck, she wondered if it was her own. A quick trip to the closet for cleaning supplies took care of it.

Then she followed instructions to turn the ride on and ran it through a practice cycle. Everything was in order by the time she opened the door to the public.

A slow trickle of people came in throughout the day. Crowds never slammed her, as they often did at the cafe. While she appreciated the slower pace, there were a few times, when she had no customers, that she felt bored.

During one of those breaks, she considered the pushback she'd taken from friends and family. Why had she fought so hard for this opportunity? Her least favorite customers to wait on at the cafe were the families with kids. While adults came in, the vast majority of riders were children.

Later in the afternoon, a little girl tripped stepping off the platform and skinned her knee. Penny hurried over to help the girl's mother. "Is she okay?"

"It's just a skinned knee, but I wish they had stairs here. It's a big step for little ones," the woman said.

The child's shoulders shook with big, muffled tears and Penny winced at the abraded skin which oozed blood. "It's okay, honey. We will get you bandaged up." She told the handful of people waiting that the ride would be briefly delayed and hurried to the supply closet.

She applied antibiotic ointment to the scrape and allowed the girl to choose her own bandage. To her relief, the girl's cries withered to hiccups. The child even cracked a small smile when she admired her Little Mermaid bandage.

The girl's mother thanked Penny and led her daughter away with the promise of stopping for ice cream on the way home. Relieved it had been nothing more serious, Penny started the ride again. She would mention the possibility of installing stairs to park management. Riders of the carousel seemed accident prone. This was her third visit to the carousel, and she'd already seen a splinter, a heart attack, and a scraped knee. Only the time she'd come with Ben had been free of blood.

Thinking of blood reminded her of the horrifying dream she'd experienced where the lion killed the antelope. But the carousel in that dream more closely resembled the carousel at the zoo. Except for the golden horse. Had the little girl been riding the golden horse? Penny couldn't remember. And what difference did it make? It wasn't an actual horse, just a wooden facsimile. Right?

She glanced over at the carousel from where she stood in the operator's booth, her gaze drawn to the tawny horse. It stood empty, this round, going up and down on its pole, its painted eyes bright and curiously lifelike. She turned her attention back to the controls.

She couldn't afford to be distracted on her first day.

***

When Penny returned Ben's car, he suggested they grab a new battery and something to eat.

"I'm not a mechanic, but I can install a battery. Besides, you still owe me a tarot reading."

They drove to an auto parts store and then went through the drive-through at a burger joint. They placed their orders, and Penny got something for Dora as well.

"The refrigerator at home is just about empty. I've been too busy to go grocery shopping." She wasn't sure who was more excited, Plato or her sister, when she entered the house with Ben, the delicious smell of burgers and fries following in their wake.

"Did you bring some for me?" Dora asked. Plato offered a whine, probably asking the same question.

Ben handed Dora a burger and fries, then looked down at Plato. "If you play your cards right, I'm sure you'll get some, too."

They dove into the hamburgers and it was almost like old times. There was only the slightest bit of tension between her and Ben and they easily buried it under chitchat about the weather, Dora's classes, Ben's clients, and Penny's new job.

After dinner, Ben went out to fix the car. He came in a few minutes later.

"That was quick," Penny said.

"You didn't need a new battery."

Feeling the start of a headache, Penny rubbed her temple. "It's not the battery? Do you have any idea what else could be wrong with it?"

"Oh, it was the battery, but somehow the wires had become disconnected. I hooked them back up, and it started right away. I don't know how much longer it will last, but you can return the one you bought today."

"That's good news." She'd dipped into her savings for another car to buy the battery. "Let's go do your reading." As she led Ben up to the hobby room, the slight tension from before coalesced into a tight knot in her belly. "I spoke to Juniper."

"How is she?"

Penny placed her deck of cards on the table and lit a few candles. "Fine. She agreed to do some research. A few days ago she sent me an email with some additional history of the carousel. After the fire at The Highlands, it spent some time with a private collector before being donated to the county. It operated at another area park before being restored and brought to Faust Park."

"And Mr. Jenkins stayed with it the whole time?"

"I think so."

"Weird."

Penny shrugged. "Maybe, but it grows on you."

"So you like the new job?"

"I do," she said firmly. After all the opposition she had faced, she wasn't about to admit to her occasional boredom or the uptake in frequency and intensity of her dreams.

"Glad it's worth it. Dora told me Gage is pretty upset with you."

Penny pressed her lips together. "Dora should mind her own business."

"She cares about you."

"Humph. Enough talk about me. What question can I answer for you today?"

"I want to know if Juniper made the right choice by joining Adam on tour."

"You know I don't read about third parties. The question has to be about you. You can ask about the future of your relationship with Juniper."

"Will we even have a relationship? What if she doesn't come home?"

"Then maybe being with Adam is the right decision for her."

"I never thought she was so shallow."

"Juniper made no secret of her feelings for you, but you didn't appear to return them. She was bound to look elsewhere, eventually. Don't you want her to be happy?"

"Of course." Ben ran his hand through his dark waves, looking uncomfortable. "You must think me a total ass. I should never have allowed you to break up with me just because Juniper dented my pride."

Penny leaned back in her chair, unsure they would even need the cards today. "Did she only hurt your pride? Or is your heart involved?"

Ben bolted from his chair and paced around the room. "We've been friends for ages. I love her, but not in that way. Or at least I don't think so."

"Now we're getting to the crux of your question. I'll do a simple, three card relationship reading." She took a deep breath to clear her mind and shuffled the cards. She needed all her concentration to maintain objectivity. Being involved in the situation, even peripherally, stretched her tarot ethics. Ben should probably use another reader, but she was the only one available right now.

After telling Ben to sit and cut the deck, she laid out three cards. "What you feel about the relationship—King of Pentacles. You feel you're in control of your relationship, and Juniper owes you some form of allegiance. That's why you are so hurt and confused by her actions. You fear you are losing her."

"You're spot on. I can't see us going back to the way things were before even if she comes to her senses and returns home."

"Is that a bad thing? Relationships grow and change."

Ben shrugged and pointed at the next card, the Five of Pentacles. "That looks ominous."

Penny nodded. "It shows how Juniper feels about the relationship. Tradition considers The Five of Pentacles a card of poverty. Juniper doesn't feel she's getting enough out of her relationship with you. It's lacking."

"She wanted more from me. She wanted us to be a couple, but I was always afraid of ruining our friendship. Maybe I should have been more daring. Adam destroyed our friendship anyway."

"Let's look at the third card. This tells where your relationship is headed. We have The Chariot reversed. It's a major arcana card representing a major life event, which makes sense because Juniper has been a major part of your life until now. Will she continue to be a major part of your life? The two of you are at a crossroads."

"Well, what's the answer?"

"It's not that easy. You and Juniper each have free will. Either of you can make the choice to cut the other out of their life. But you can just as easily make the choice to extend your relationship, although it may be different now. Since the card is reversed, I think you're undecided which direction to take."

"I don't see how we can remain friends if she continues to be a rock star's arm candy."

Penny shuffled the three cards back into the deck. "You seem convinced that Juniper and Adam don't have feelings for each other. That she only wants him for fame and money and he only wants her for her beauty and photo ops. What if they are in love?"

Ben frowned. "Do you think they're in love?"

"Why do you think they're not?"

Ben put his elbows on the table and rested his head in his hands. "They seem so different."

"Opposites attract."

"Maybe." He lifted his head, but still looked defeated. "I guess I should give them the benefit of the doubt."

"I think you should if you want to keep Juniper as part of your life. For what it's worth, you didn't have any cups in your reading. Cups are the suit of emotions. I know you care deeply for Juniper, but I'm not convinced you're in love with her."

Chapter 10

B ack at work the next day, Penny did a brief experiment. If Gage was right and her annoyance at being forced to cook that day at the cafe had somehow transferred to the food, she wondered if she could produce the opposite effect on purpose.

During one break in the crowd, when no one was riding, she listened to an upbeat song on her phone. When the next group of people came in, she tried to infuse her sense of wellbeing into the controls, thinking about how the music had made her feel as she pushed the lever.

The ride ran as normal, but she monitored the kids, trying to see if they appeared more excited than usual. The kids, and even the adults, always seemed charmed by the old-fashioned ride, but with modern-day roller coasters that went upside down, rides that fell from dizzying heights, and lifelike animation, she knew the carousel couldn't really compete. Still, parents could bring their kids for a picnic in the park and a ride on the carousel for a fraction of the price of going to a theme park.

She couldn't really tell any difference in the behavior of the kids, but at least no one fell and got injured. She wasn't sure why she felt such an attachment to the job, but she wanted to stay on for the full two weeks. She'd been in contact with Mr. Jenkins and he planned to be back by then, but she didn't know if his doctors agreed.

She was running the last ride for the day, eager to get home and do some online tarot readings, when one kid got off the horse, stumbled as if he was dizzy, and then vomited all over the platform. Nearby riders jumped out of the way, one crying out in disgust.

Penny hurried over, her own stomach rebelling. She helped the little boy off the platform and into the care of his mother, who looked horrified.

"I'm sorry, he rarely gets motion sickness."

"Do you think he's getting sick?" Penny hoped not. Stomach flu was very contagious and a bout would take her out of the game for a couple of days.

"I don't think so, but you never know what germs they pick up at school. I'd better take him straight home."

Penny ushered all the remaining patrons out, taking a deep breath of the crisp outdoor air before locking the door behind them. Then she went to the closet to get supplies for tackling the mess.

At last she finished. She washed her hands several times in the bathroom, hoping to rid them of any lingering viruses. It was just a boy coming down with something. Or extremely sensitive to motion sickness. She was sure it had nothing to do with her trying to add a bit more "oomph" to the ride.

Well, almost sure.

As she was closing the storage closet, she noticed something on the shelf behind a roll of paper towels. She moved the paper towels so she could see it more clearly. It was a small knife, almost like a scalpel. She ran her finger along the blade, jerking back at the sting. A drop of blood welled up on the pad of her finger. The blade was very sharp.

As if in a daze, Penny grabbed the knife by its handle and walked over to the carousel. The ride was dark and quiet without the sparkling lights and music. All the horses were still, some frozen at the top of their loop while others hovered midway or rested near the floor.

The golden horse where she had gotten her splinter called to her. She went to it and rubbed her injured finger over the horse's muzzle. It left a trace of blood. Still moving mechanically, as if she were a puppet on strings, she ran the blade along her arm, deep enough to draw blood, but not so deep as to cause serious harm. She held her arm over the horse, watching in fascination as blood dripped from the cut to the brightly painted wood. The ruby-red drops gleamed for a moment under the fluorescent lights, before the wood sucked them up like rain on the desert ground.

Penny's arm stung, drawing her back into herself. She gazed down at the ugly red line which ran down her forearm. It was no longer bleeding, but still hurt. Had she cut herself?

Her other hand held a knife. She had a vague memory of pressing the blade against her skin. Why would she do that? Now she would have blood to clean up, too.

But she could find no trace of blood on the carousel. If it wasn't for the mark on her arm, she might have thought she imagined the whole thing. What was she doing with a knife, anyway?

She returned the knife to the closet and grabbed a bandage from the first aid kit. She covered her wound, locked up, and walked out to her car. Since she'd wasted time cleaning up after the boy, she was going to be late getting home.

What a strange day.

***

Archie Jenkins checked out of his hotel room. There was no point in hanging around any longer. His dad was on the mend and his half-hearted attempt to get Penny fired from the carousel job had failed. Perhaps he should have done actual damage to her car, not just disconnect the battery. But it wasn't like he needed the job. He could go back to his old one or get something new. There were always plenty of teens eager to work at theme parks and a fair number of retirees, too, but it was tough to find someone long-term. The teens would take off for college in a few years and retirees were likely to get sick. Look at his dad.

But Archie's employment record wasn't exactly spotless. He'd job hopped over the years, but this gave him experience with parks all across the country.

Seeing his father again hadn't been exactly what he was expecting. The tall, fit man he remembered had shrunk to a thin, pale copy. He'd lost track of how many years had passed since he ran away from The Highlands. The possibility that his dad would die in the blaze, too stubborn to leave his beloved carousel, had terrified him.

He'd listened to the news and soon learned there had been no fatalities, but he'd been so angry with his father, he hadn't wanted to return. So he'd struck out on his own, doing the carnival circuit until he graduated to theme parks. It hadn't been easy, but at the time he'd feared that if he stayed with his old man, he'd be destined to walk the same path, wasting his life on a hunk of wood.

Instead, although he'd followed his father into the entertainment industry, he'd traveled across the country and worked every type of ride out there. He'd even worked in various theme park restaurants, but he preferred working with the machinery. He supposed he got his love of gears and motors from his dad.

He stopped by the nursing home to say goodbye. Once he'd thought to gloat and rub in how much his dad had lost by choosing the carousel over his family and forcing his only son to run away. But as he looked down at Elliot's frail body, it didn't seem worth it. The knowledge was there in the old man's tired eyes, anyway.

"I'm gonna take off. Can't expect the theme park to hold my job forever when the busy season is just around the corner."

"Thanks for coming, son. I'm sorry if you feel I pushed you away all those years ago. I just wanted you to understand how important this job is. It's our family legacy."

"Then why give it to that girl? You don't even know her. You don't owe her anything. It was the sister who saved your life."

"I didn't know how to find you. Didn't know for sure if you were even still alive."

Archie cleared his throat. "I sent a few postcards."

"And I still have them all. But it's been over a year since I received one."

"Why not retire and let the park service find someone to replace you?"

His dad shook his head. "I can't do that. The carousel is too much responsibility. She liked Penny. I could tell."

"It, not she. You talk about that stupid carousel like it's a person. Grandpa might have carved that yellow horse, but it's just wood and metal, wires and gears."

"You know it's not. Her spirit lives on in the horse your grandfather carved. And it's our duty to serve her."

Irritated, Archie stood. "Well, I gotta go. But when you retire for real, keep me in mind. It's time I settled down in one location." If he had a steady job, maybe he would even marry, start a family. Or not. It might be nice to have a steady girlfriend, but he didn't want to bother with kids. If he could find a woman. Since he was middle-aged and nearly broke, most women weren't interested.

"Stay in touch. I'd be happy to keep the job in the family." Elliot didn't quite meet his son's eyes, and Archie thought he detected a hint of doubt in his words. Did the old man actually think he couldn't handle a simple carousel when he'd worked some of the fastest roller coasters in the world? He stalked off to the elevators.

Not really wanting to deal with the jerk who had almost fired him, Archie had considered applying at Six Flags and staying near his dad. Now he wanted nothing more than to get in his car and drive all the way to California. But he'd worked in California before and it was too expensive to make it on a theme park salary. Florida would be far enough. Or maybe he should just knuckle under to his supervisor and go back to his old job. He had a decent apartment there and a handful of friends.

The elevator still hadn't come, and he pushed the button again. What was taking so long? The building only had three floors.

"Screw it." His skin crawled at the wait. Why had he even considered staying? He couldn't wait to put his hometown in his rear-view mirror. He headed for the stairs. Might as well stretch his legs before the long drive.

The stairwell was utilitarian, with concrete walls and cheap linoleum on the floor. His steps echoed hollowly on the treads. He hit the landing of the second floor and pushed on. Two steps down, he tripped. He grabbed for the rail, but his momentum carried him forward and broke the weak hold of his fingers. He tumbled down the rest of the way like a crash test dummy, striking his head on the edge of the stair. A scream tore from his mouth, the sound bouncing around the concrete walls. When he reached the bottom, he didn't move.

***

When Penny received a text from Gage on Monday, her day off, she almost didn't open it. She expected he wanted her to come in to the cafe since she wasn't busy with the carousel. To her surprise, he asked nothing of the sort.

Gage: **I've been a jerk. I'd like to apologize. Can I come over?**
Penny: **Sure. I'm home.**

She set the phone down as butterflies blossomed in her belly. She didn't want her new job to come between them. In fact, one reason she'd considered the position was to avoid the employee/boss issue. She'd spent her extra free time working on her tarot business and had grown her list of newsletter subscribers. Some of them would surely decide to book a reading and become regular customers. Even if the park job didn't work out long term, she might eventually read tarot full-time.

It was what she had longed to do when she first discovered tarot and her talent for the cards in high school. Her grandmother had even encouraged her. But she'd lost faith when she failed to predict Dora's car accident. Her confidence had grown since moving to Little Hills and taking up tarot again, but the thought of leaving the carousel, a job she'd only held for a week, tugged at her heart. She'd grown used to the music and often hummed the tune beneath her breath even when she was at home. The dreams robbed her of sleep, but she hoped they would subside with time.

Plato went crazy when Gage knocked on the door. Her boss ruffled the dog's head and suggested they sit outside. "It's a nice day."

Penny pulled a couple sodas from the fridge, and they took them out to the patio. Gage threw a ball for Plato, and the dog took off after it.

"I'm sorry I was such a jerk about your job. I grew up in the restaurant business and understand why you would want to escape it. I shouldn't have tried to stand in your way."

"I should have given you more notice. We were both at fault, but I want to be friends again." She wanted to be more than friends, but didn't want to push.

"You're my best waitress. And I enjoy having you around all day."

"I'll be back in another week."

"How's it going?"

"Great." If she didn't count the scraped knee, the barf, and the sleepless nights. Plato brought her the ball and she threw it.

"Want to go out to lunch?"

Penny agreed, hoping she didn't sound too eager.

"You choose the place this time."

"Well, I've been wanting to go to this park." She told him the name. "We could pick up sandwiches on the way."

Gage looked the park up on his phone. "It's way down south. Why this one?"

"It's where the carousel used to operate before the county restored it and moved it to Faust Park. I thought seeing its previous home might give me some more insight."

"Insight into what?"

Penny shrugged. "It was a dumb idea. We can go somewhere closer."

Gage cocked his head to one side. "No, I don't mind the drive. Let's check it out."

Penny packed up some more sodas, bottled water, and chips. They put Plato in the car and stopped by a sub shop. Then Gage drove them to Sylvan Springs. They ate their picnic at the pavilion before walking Plato around the park. A few younger kids played on the playground, but since school was in session, only a few teens were using the skate park.

"Do you think they're skipping school or are they older than they look?" Penny asked.

A smile tugged at Gage's lips. "Definitely playing hooky. Did it myself a time or two."

Penny had never been brave enough to skip class. She had a hard enough time fitting in and passing her classes with the number of times she moved. This was a playful side of Gage she had not seen before. "So what did you do when you played hooky?"

"This mostly." Gage gestured towards the skateboarders. "I was pretty good back in the day, but I'd probably break my neck now if I got on a board. What about you?"

"Never skipped school by choice, but I missed plenty of days since we moved around a lot." Gage knew her father was in prison, but she hadn't shared many details of her childhood. Now that she thought about it, neither had Gage. "I wouldn't have taken you for a skateboarder."

"I was a bit of a rebel. Skateboarding fit right in with my smoking, drinking, and long hair." Gage still wore his hair longer than average.

"I've sampled your whiskey stash, but I've never seen you smoke."

"Quit about ten years ago. It's a hard habit to break, so it's better to never start."

"I had a friend who taught me how to smoke, but lucky for me, I didn't like the taste."

"Some friend."

"I think she meant well."

They walked past the tennis courts. A couple of older women occupied one court, but the other was empty. The spray fountain play area wasn't open yet.

"Thanks for bringing me out here. I don't really know what I expected to find. I don't even know where the carousel stood when it was here."

"It was nice to have a picnic before it gets too hot and I'd have loved to have had a skating area like this when I was a teenager."

As they headed back to the car, they passed the shelter where they had eaten lunch. An old man sat at a table, his legs stretched out before him. Penny nodded at him, and then on an impulse stopped. Plato sniffed at the man's pant legs. "Were you familiar with this park when the carousel was here?"

"Sure. I've lived around here all my life. Rode the carousel many times and even took my kids to it." He gave in to Plato's subtle pressure and patted the dog on the head.

"I work at its new location."

"I was mad at first when they moved it, but I'm glad it's gone. Made the park more peaceful. I just wish they hadn't built the skate park. Attracts gangs."

Penny didn't know if there was any truth to the old man's complaint, but she saw Gage smother a smile. "Have a good day." She tugged on the leash to get Plato to leave his new friend.

"Be careful."

"How so?"

The man pressed his lips together and looked like he wished he'd kept his mouth shut. "The carousel would often break down and kids tripped and fell. But things are probably better now that they fixed it up. And we get far worse injuries at the skate park. My granddaughter went rollerblading there and broke her arm."

"Thanks." They continued on their way, Penny feeling a tad uneasy. Could the carousel be cursed? At least the old man had said nothing about it being haunted.

They reached the car, boosted Plato into the back seat, and buckled up. Gage pulled out into traffic. "I know I said I would not interfere anymore, but I'll be glad when you finish up this temporary post. The carousel doesn't seem to have the best track record."

"Then I only have one more week to figure out what's wrong. If anything is wrong. You haven't even seen how beautiful it is."

"I'll stop by sometime this week."

Warmth pooled in her belly and stole up her cheeks, forcing out the chill left by the old man's words. Something was wrong with the carousel. She knew it deep inside. But it still held a fascination for her, perhaps similar to what had drawn Gage to act out as a youth. The lure of the dangerous and unknown. For once she wanted to throw caution to the wind and live on the edge for a while.

Chapter 11

When Archie came to, his head felt like someone had taken a bat to it. His entire body hurt, and he moaned as hands straightened his splayed limbs.

"Stay calm, we're going to take care of you," a female voice said.

He pried his eyes open, then shut them again as the light stabbed at his eyeballs. He lay at the foot of some stairs. What was he doing here? The last thing he remembered was leaving his dad's room, prepared to suck up to his boss if it got him his job back.

"On three," someone said and hands lifted him onto a stretcher. They wheeled him out into the parking lot where an ambulance waited.

"We're taking you to the hospital."

"What happened?"

"Someone found you in the stairwell. You must have fallen down the stairs."

Why would he have taken the stairs? Although he wasn't crazy about the closed confines of elevators, it was better than wasting energy schlepping it on the stairs. Someone must have pushed him. But how had that person lured him into the stairwell?

It was a brief trip to the hospital and soon he was in the emergency room where a team of health workers asked him his name as they examined him. A doctor shined a light into his eyes and then gave him the verdict.

"You're a lucky man, Archie. No broken bones. You hit your head hard, though, so we're going to watch you overnight. We've given you something for the pain, so you should feel better soon."

Archie felt the drug filtering through his bloodstream, taking the edge off the throbbing in his head and the overall aching of his body. Good thing his boss hadn't actually fired him, so he still had his health insurance. But he couldn't catch a break. He was going to lose a few more days of work, and his supervisor would use any excuse to get rid of him.

His jerk of a supervisor put him on probation and then a red-headed twit had stolen his family job out from under him. Now this. Nothing had gone right since hearing about his father's heart attack.

Bad luck had dogged him since the dreaded carousel came back into his life.

He'd hated the thing as a child. Hated how his dad preferred to spend his time polishing the already shining wood and pandering to other people's children rather than his own son.

He hadn't planned to set The Highlands alight, but when the grease fire started in the kitchen, he'd seized his opportunity. He'd tipped the burning skillet over and watched in fascinated delight as the flames leaped up the wall and ignited the old, dry wood.

But what had initially been beautiful, a bright bonfire of color, had spread quickly. By the time flames engulfed the kitchen, nearby structures were already alight. Someone called the fire department, but it was clear the fire had too big a head start. Frightened, he'd run to the carousel where his dad worked.

His dad helped evacuate the customers, but refused to leave the carousel.

"Come on, Dad," Archie cried. "The whole place is going up in flames. We need to get out of here."

"You go. I can't leave her."

"Are you crazy? The fire department told everyone to get out. Are you going to die for this hunk of junk?"

"Calm down, Archie. The fire is concentrated on the other side of the park. I don't think we're in any danger here, but if it comes closer, I'm prepared." He pulled a handsaw out of his locker. "I will cut her loose and make my escape."

By "her" Archie knew he meant the yellow horse carved by his grandfather. "Come on, Dad. It's not worth it."

His father drew him close and clapped him on the back. "Go on, now. Nothing is going to happen to me, but if it does, you need to carry on the family legacy."

Archie couldn't believe his ears. His father was choosing the carousel again, over his son and even over his own safety. He said nothing, but as he backed away from his father, pressure built in his chest. His father had made his priorities clear. Archie would do the same. If his father didn't come with him now, he vowed never to return to the amusement park.

He'd kept that promise. He ran away, expecting to never return. The fire destroyed The Highlands, although, as his father had predicted, the carousel survived relatively unharmed. He'd been happy to hear The Highlands closed, but when he'd learned his father was still caring for the carousel, now in some stupid park, he'd cut all ties and began wandering around the country.

He should never have allowed himself to be called back. The carousel was clearly dangerous.

He spent the rest of the day in the hospital, watching TV and enjoying having all his meals brought to him. The food wasn't very good, but at least he didn't have to cook.

By the time he woke up the next morning, boredom was setting in and he looked forward to getting out of the hospital. The carousel had a beef with him, but he figured he would be safe now that he was on guard. His idiot bosses treated him like he was stupid since he'd never finished high school, but he was smart enough and had learned far more in the school of hard knocks than he'd ever learned in the classroom. He could outsmart a block of wood.

A pretty young nurse brought his breakfast, and he gave her the once over. She placed the tray on his table and hurried out of the room.

As he ate his eggs and toast, Archie considered whether he should visit his dad one last time. They'd already said their goodbyes, but he could warn him the carousel was stepping up its game. His father knew the thing was powerful, even if he didn't seem to realize it was evil. That's why he had kept close to it all these years.

When the doctor came in, he had a solemn look on his face. Archie felt a flash of irritation. What now? He wanted to be discharged. His head still hurt, but he felt better than yesterday.

"Mr. Jenkins, I'm afraid I have some bad news."

Archie groaned. They'd taken some blood for tests. What if they'd discovered he had cancer or something? His heart rate accelerated. Surely the horse didn't have that kind of power. "What?"

"After the paramedics brought you to the hospital, staff at the nursing home told your father about your accident. They assured him you were conscious, coherent, and likely to make a full recovery, but your father grew agitated. They had to sedate him."

"But he's okay, right?" Conflicting emotions warred within him. While it pleased him that his dad finally seemed to be concerned about him after years of neglect, anxiety clawed at his insides. He'd not had to worry about anybody except himself in years, and the sensation felt as strange as it was unwelcome.

"I'm sorry. When the sedative wore off, your father tried to leave the nursing home. We think he might have wanted to visit you. He had another heart attack and died a few hours ago."

No! Archie closed his eyes. How could this have happened just as circumstances reunited them?

"Is there someone we can call for you? I will discharge you today, but you need to take it easy."

"There's no one." He should have reached out to his father sooner. Had he and his dad been in contact, he would have come as soon as he heard about the first heart attack. His father would not have had a chance to cozy up to the redhead. Archie would run the carousel, and his dad would still be alive.

"Just get me out of here. I've got things to do."

They would pay for their interference. The girl would pay, and so would the carousel. After all these years, that horse would get what it deserved.

***

Penny had expected to delay her visit to Jackson, the drummer of Hyperbolic, until after her return to the cafe, since Mondays were her only day off while running the carousel. But serendipity stepped in. Adam's band and Hyperbolic were sharing the stage at a weekend festival in Indiana and had enough flex in their schedule to stay over until Monday. Penny planned to drive out after she closed on Sunday night.

She'd offered to bring Dora along since her sister was a big fan of Adam and wanted a chance to meet Jackson as well. Juniper had asked if she could invite Ben, and Penny had agreed. She hadn't expected him to accept, but he'd surprised her. She hoped he had taken her advice and stopped being jealous of Juniper and Adam's relationship.

She'd planned on just the three of them, but when she mentioned the trip to Gage, he wanted to tag along. It would be close quarters with the four of them and their luggage in her little car, but Penny was looking forward to the road trip. The thought of packing up a car used to make her feel sick, but now that she had a home to come back to, she could see the allure of the road.

She rushed through her closing duties while still doing a thorough job. Her muscles tensed as she approached the golden horse, but although she put extra elbow grease into shining her up, she felt no urge to hurt herself. She still didn't understand what had caused her to behave so strangely the other day, but blamed it on the stress of cleaning up after that little boy. Every time she recalled her glimpse of Mr. Jenkins' scarred arms, she pushed the memory aside.

She got gas on the way home so she would have a full tank. They would stop somewhere for a late dinner, but shouldn't have to fuel up again until the trip home.

Dora's friend, Julie, was going to stay at their house to take care of Plato and although she pouted over missing out on hanging with rock stars, she was looking forward to time away from the dorms. She had confided to Dora that she wished she could afford an apartment. She got along with her roommate, but wanted more privacy.

Everyone was already there and waiting for her when she got home. Penny gave last-minute instructions to Julie, trying to ignore Plato's sad little face. Somehow, the dog knew he wasn't coming along this time. They stowed their bags in the trunk, and Ben offered to drive first.

"I'll get us across the river. After we stop to eat, someone else can take over."

Penny was happy to hand over the keys since she was tired from work and Dora preferred not to drive in the dark, except for short distances. She still sometimes had nightmares about the crash that had taken her hearing. She crawled into the back seat with her sister, allowing the guys to have the front.

After they crossed the river into Illinois, they began looking for a place to eat. They argued over various possibilities until Ben took the matter into his own hands.

"I'm starving. We're getting off at the next exit with food no matter what." They passed a sign showing a handful of fast-food restaurants and he put on his blinker. He pulled onto the exit ramp and barreled towards the stop sign.

"Hey dude, slow down," Gage said.

"I can't. The brakes aren't working."

Penny felt Dora stiffen beside her. "Try again."

"Nothing." Ben's voice was tight. They had, at most, seconds before they tore through the intersection and into traffic.

"Pull off the road," Gage said.

Ben jerked the wheel, and the car sailed off the pavement and onto the grass. They bounced along as Ben struggled for control.

"Watch that tree!"

Ben turned sharply, and the car fishtailed, missing the tree by inches and skidding to a halt. Ben lay his head on the steering wheel and swore under his breath.

Dora shook. Penny put her arms around her. "We're okay. We're okay." She rubbed her sister's back as Dora took deep, shuddering breaths. "We are okay, right?" She looked to the front seat.

"I'm fine, but I think Ben's had a bit of a shock," Gage said. "You're not hurt, are you?"

"No." Ben didn't lift his head. "I could have killed us all."

"It's not your fault the brakes failed," Gage said. He looked over his shoulder at Penny. "It's rare for brakes to fail without warning. Have they been giving you any trouble? Squeaking or shuddering?"

Penny shook her head. "I've had no trouble at all except for the battery coming disconnected."

Gage frowned. "We need to call a tow truck, but I'll take a look." He got out of the car and gestured for Ben to release the hood. Penny pulled out her phone and searched for a nearby towing service.

"Someone should be here in a few minutes." Seeing that Dora appeared calmer, Penny stepped out of the car. Gage was looking at the engine. "See anything?"

"You're leaking brake fluid. That's why the brakes failed."

Penny knew little about cars, even though she had dated a mechanic. "How did that happen?"

Gage pulled his head out from under the car and clambered to his feet. "Not sure, but there should have been signs things were off. You noticed nothing?"

"No, but so long as the car gets me to my destination, I pay little attention to it."

"You had trouble with your battery earlier?"

"Yes, I thought it was dead, but Ben discovered the wires had come loose."

Gage shot her a quick glance. "Wires rarely just come loose."

"I never fool around with the engine and don't think Dora would either."

"I'm not accusing you of anything. I'm just wondering if someone could have tampered with your car."

"We don't have a garage, so we park on the street. It's certainly possible. But why?"

"Good question."

"Ron's still in jail, isn't he?"

"As far as I know."

"I can't think of anyone else who has it out for me. Well, except maybe for Mr. Jenkins' son, Archie. He expected the carousel job to be his."

"Disconnecting your battery is more of a prank. Disabling the brakes put all our lives at risk. It seems a stretch. What is so special about this part-time gig? You were happy to ditch me and the cafe for it and now this guy will *kill* for it? Something isn't right."

"I thought you had forgiven me for taking a leave of absence without notice," Penny muttered.

"I have, but it was out of character. And I can't believe any right-minded person would risk a murder charge to get a minimum wage job when every fast-food joint you pass has a help wanted sign."

"It pays a lot better than minimum wage. I work fewer hours and make almost as much as I do at the cafe." Flashing lights grabbed her attention. "The tow truck is here."

She went to meet the driver and arranged for the car to be towed to the nearest garage. "But how will we get to town? Should I call a rideshare?"

"I can give you a lift to a motel if you don't mind being crowded," the truck driver said.

"Thanks." She had hoped to reach their destination late tonight, sleep in, and be ready to meet with Jackson tomorrow. Obviously that would not happen. The garage had closed hours ago, and she didn't know for sure they could even get to her car tomorrow. She would have to cancel the reading. It wouldn't do her reputation any good, but hopefully he would understand.

It would disappoint Dora to miss seeing Adam and Jackson and Ben would lose his chance to patch things up with Juniper. But without a car, Penny didn't see they had any choice.

She shared the plan with the others, and they crammed into the cab of the tow truck. Dora sat on Ben's lap, and Penny sat on Gage's.

"Which motel?" The driver listed off the choices.

Gage picked one, and the driver dropped them off in the parking lot. "The garage will be in touch with you tomorrow."

They checked in at the front desk, choosing a double queen room. Penny didn't mind sleeping with her sister, but suspected the guys might be uncomfortable about sharing a bed. No one, however, wanted to spring for a second room.

"I'm still hungry," Ben announced as they brought their bags into the room. "Why don't we order a couple of pizzas?"

"You guys take care of dinner. I need to let Juniper know we won't be arriving tonight. And tell Jackson we need to reschedule." Penny curled up in an armchair, trying to ignore the others' squabbling voices. She sent a brief, professional email to Jackson, explaining she'd experienced car trouble and wouldn't be able to keep their appointment unless the garage could fix her car first thing in the morning.

Then she went into the bathroom and called Juniper.

"Hi, Penny. What's going on? Are you stopped for dinner?"

"Stopped for the night, I'm afraid. Car trouble."

"Will you still be coming in tomorrow?"

"Depends how quickly they can fix my car."

"Probably should have taken Ben's car." Juniper sounded disappointed.

"Yes, especially since this is the second problem I've had this week. Gage thinks someone might have tampered with it."

"Really? Like a teenager on a dare?"

"More like someone trying to mess with me."

Juniper was quiet for a moment. "You think it has something to do with your latest case?"

"I don't know. It's not really even a case. We haven't confirmed any haunting. But it made the operator's son mad when I temporarily got the job he expected would be his. I don't have any proof, but I wouldn't put it past him to get rid of me."

"I wasn't able to find much about the carousel, but there are plenty of tales of haunted objects. Usually dolls or puppets."

Penny shivered. "I played with dolls as a kid, but puppets give me the creeps."

"Call me tomorrow once you know your schedule. If we can't get together, I'll email you what I have about haunted dolls. I don't know if it will be any help, but it can't hurt."

Penny heard a knock on the main door, and the tantalizing smell of pizza drifted into the bathroom. "Gotta go. Dinner's here." She put her phone away and joined the others. At the rate they were grabbing slices, she needed to get some before it was all gone.

As she ate, she considered Juniper's words. Could this be a case of a haunted object? Could the spirit of a horse inhabit the carousel? She'd heard of animal hauntings, usually dogs or cats, but had no experience with them.

And nothing Juniper had said explained why she'd dripped blood on the horse. She had told no one about that since it sounded crazy, even to her.

She also worried about her calm acceptance of the accident. They could have been seriously hurt, even killed, and she didn't have extra money in the budget for costly repairs. But the interruption of their journey relieved her. The sooner she got back to the carousel, the better.

Chapter 12

When Penny awoke the next morning, she had a couple of messages. One was from the garage telling her they hoped to have her car fixed by the end of the day. The second was from Juniper. She explained that since the accident had stranded Penny, Jackson wanted to come to her. Juniper was hitching a ride with him.

Penny told the others about the change in plans. They took turns getting ready in the bathroom and reconvened in the breakfast room where the motel served a free breakfast.

Ben went for a walk. "Might as well get some pictures while I'm here." He worked as a professional photographer and also took artistic photos when he got the chance.

"I'll work on homework until Jackson gets here." While disappointed Adam wouldn't be coming, Dora still looked forward to meeting the famous drummer.

"That leaves us," Gage said. "I'll go check out the competition in town and see if I can get any new ideas for the cafe. You're welcome to come with me."

Penny declined. "I need to prepare for my meeting with Jackson. Having a celebrity for a client could do wonders for my tarot business."

"Sure, I get it." Gage dumped his trash and left the motel. Left alone with Dora, Penny hoped Gage hadn't taken offense at yet more evidence that she eventually wanted to leave his employ.

"You know how to clear a room," Dora said.

"Yeah, well, this trip isn't turning out quite like I had hoped. Are you doing okay?"

"Why wouldn't I be?"

"We were in a car accident yesterday. It had to have brought back memories."

"I thought I might have a heart attack when it looked like Ben was going to crash into a tree, but nobody got hurt. I'm fine."

Penny studied her sister. Dora's hand trembled slightly as she set down her teacup. "I'm here if you need to talk."

Dora waved her away. "Go do whatever you need to do to get ready. I'm going to bring my books down to the lounge and study."

Penny went up to the hotel room, appreciating that the others had all given her privacy. She meditated for fifteen minutes and then consulted a few tarot books she'd brought with her. Not knowing exactly what Jackson wanted to know, she didn't choose a spread yet, but considered a few options.

When Jackson and Juniper arrived an hour later, she was ready. Juniper introduced them and then left to find Ben.

Penny told Jackson to take a seat. Her voice sounded shaky, which annoyed her. Famous or not, he was just a guy. A handsome guy, tall, with long blond hair and capable hands. She guessed they got a workout banging away at the drums.

But a guy who also displayed signs of nervousness as he plopped into the desk chair and cracked his prominent knuckles.

Penny immediately felt more at ease, as if his nervousness canceled out her own. Jackson was here for her help, and it was her responsibility to do what she could for him. She asked him a few warm-up questions as she lit her candles. Then she got down to business.

"Do you have a specific question or do you want me to do a more general reading?"

"I want to know whether I should leave Hyperbolic and go out on my own."

Penny explained it wasn't her job to tell him what to do, but to show him the pros and cons of each possibility. "You have free will and the decisions you make create your future. Not the cards."

"But you're psychic. Adam told me you were."

"Yes..." she dragged out the word. "My readings are accurate, almost as if I am sometimes privy to information I have no rational reason for knowing. I'm not sure I'm psychic, but I don't need to be. Any intuitive person can learn how to interpret the cards."

Jackson appeared satisfied with her explanation, and they continued. She went with a traditional Celtic Cross spread and in the end suggested he speak with the other band members about taking a greater creative role within the group. She advised he only quit if they refused to allow him to stretch his wings.

Jackson thanked her, paid her the highest fee she'd ever received, since it included travel costs, and agreed to meet Dora.

"Thanks, she'll be thrilled."

Dora came up to the room, and Jackson signed an autograph for her. Penny texted Gage, Ben, and Juniper telling them she'd finished the reading and they all agreed to meet at an old style diner Gage had discovered. Penny checked out of the hotel and stowed their bags with bell service before Jackson drove them over in his car.

The place boasted lots of glass and chrome and looked like the owners had transported it from the 1950s. They sat in a booth and ordered burgers, fries, and milkshakes. Their waitress glanced twice at

Jackson, but either decided to give him his privacy or was unsure if she recognized him, because she said nothing.

"Juniper filled me in about haunted dolls," Ben said. "If an evil spirit possesses the carousel, I might not have picked up on it."

"Give us the scoop," Gage said.

"There are several stories of haunted dolls. One of the most famous is Robert. It was part of the inspiration behind the Chucky doll from the *Child's Play* movie. Gene, the boy who owned him, would blame the doll for breaking things, and his family heard him talking to Robert. Neighbors claimed the doll would watch them from the windows. Some people said the doll moved on its own and understood conversations held in its presence. It's now in a museum, but continues to exert an evil influence. Signs warn visitors not to insult Robert because he might curse them with bad luck."

"Is there an explanation for how or why the doll can do this?" Gage asked.

"Not really, but according to tradition, a voodoo practitioner gave Gene the toy."

"Any connection between the carousel and voodoo?"

"Not that I found," Juniper said.

"Me neither," Penny confirmed.

"Tell them about the Raggedy Ann doll," Dora said. "It creeped me out because I remember you used to have one of those dolls."

"I loved that doll," Penny protested. The doll had survived many moves and by the time Penny finally discarded her, she had lived up to her name.

"There is this other Raggedy Ann doll, named Annabelle, who would supposedly leave notes for its owner and her roommate begging for help. Then the roommate's fiancé claimed the doll attacked him and tried to choke him. The girls contacted a medium who claimed the spirit of a dead girl haunted the doll."

"So something trapped a ghost in the doll's body," Gage said.

"That was one explanation. But the paranormal experts who now own the doll and display it in their museum say it's controlled by a dark entity."

"Like a demon."

Juniper nodded.

"So, the carousel could be haunted by a dead person or possessed by a demon," Gage said.

"Or none of the above," Penny said. "I don't think the carousel is evil." *Despite its taste for blood.* She repressed a shiver. A nagging anxiety tugged at her and she wished she'd postponed the road trip until after her tenure at the carousel. It didn't feel right being so far away.

"Well, as we've learned in our other cases, ghosts aren't necessarily evil. They may just have their own agenda," Ben said.

Jackson finally joined the conversation. "This is cool. When you told me your friend read tarot cards and could help me with some problems I was having, I didn't expect to meet the Scooby Gang."

Juniper flipped her dark, straight hair over her shoulder. "Just because I'm a boring librarian doesn't mean I don't know interesting people. I hang out with rock stars and paranormal investigators."

"Hey, I never called you boring," Jackson protested.

Penny's phone rang, and she glanced down at the display. "Sorry, it's the park service. I need to take this." She walked away from the table, her unease growing. Something was wrong. She felt it like a rock in her gut. The carousel was closed today. What could have happened?

"Hello, this is Penny."

"Penny, sorry to call on your day off, but there has been an unfortunate development."

"What?" Penny forced the word past the tightness in her chest. She thought about The Highlands going up in flames long before she was born. Could the building housing the carousel have caught fire?

"Mr. Jenkins had another heart attack. He didn't survive this time."

"Oh, no." She barely knew the man, but her eyes grew moist. He'd been so kind to her.

"I'm sorry. I know you were friends. He spoke so highly of you."

Why? He had barely known her, either.

"He passed a few days ago, but we just found out when his son inquired about taking on the position. I know you only took a leave of absence from your current job, but I wanted to offer the job to you first if you are interested."

"I'm interested," she said before thinking it over or talking to Gage or Dora. If she didn't jump on the job now, they might give Archie the job. She would deal with the fallout later.

***

Juniper and Jackson left after lunch. The others hung around the hotel lobby until the garage called and told them the car was ready.

Dora cried when Penny told her Mr. Jenkins was dead.

"Julie and I saved his life, but it was all for nothing."

"Never think that. He was an old man and perhaps it was his time to go, but by saving him you gave him the chance to reconcile with his son." Penny didn't admire the younger Jenkins man, but she'd seen the pride and happiness on Elliot's face when he introduced them. "What you gave him was priceless."

Dora managed a watery smile. "Are you okay? He really liked you."

"He was a sweet old guy, but I'm fine." Penny wasn't sure she spoke the truth. Gage had been glaring at her ever since she told the others what had happened. They had just rekindled their romance, and now she was letting him down again. But the pull she felt towards the carousel was overwhelming. She wouldn't be able to relax until they returned home.

Gage insisted on driving, and Penny didn't argue. She got in back and Dora crawled in after her, trying to hide her clenched fists.

Penny touched her sister's shoulder. "I had them do a full inspection on the car and fix the brakes. Everything should be fine."

They drove home without incident, Dora even dozing off after a while. The men left shortly after they arrived back at Penny and Dora's house, but Penny pulled Gage aside first.

"I'm sorry about this. Everything happened so quickly. I thought I would have more time, but I'm willing to work every Monday until you can find a replacement."

"I'm not mad about you leaving the cafe. Sure, it's going to be hard to replace you, but that's not why I'm upset."

"Then what?"

"I'm worried. Have you forgotten the haunted doll stories Juniper shared with us? The dreams alone were worrisome, but now someone connected to the carousel has died."

"He was an old man with a heart condition."

"Still."

"I appreciate your concern, but everything will be fine."

Gage didn't smile, but the line across his forehead smoothed out. "I'll call you tomorrow."

Plato was glad to see his owners, although Julie swore she'd spoiled him rotten.

"Ungrateful," she said, stroking him behind the ears. "See if I ever pet sit for you again." She looked up at Dora and Penny. "Just kidding. I'd totally do it again."

Dora invited Julie to stay the night. Penny thought it a good idea, since she worried her sister might still be upset about the accident. And the girls could comfort each other since Mr. Jenkins' death also saddened Julie. "Just don't stay up too late. You have school tomorrow."

"Yes, Mom." Dora rolled her eyes.

Penny ignored her and went up to her room, leaving the girls control of the TV. Tomorrow would be a big day. Responsibility for the carousel was now all hers.

***

Despite her misgivings and excitement from the night before, Penny's first day as official operator of the carousel was uneventful. An employee from human resources met her at the building before opening, and Penny signed new paperwork.

The carousel opened on time, and a steady stream of customers came through. No one got hurt or sick. One mother was rude, but Penny was used to dealing with troublesome people.

After closing, she swept the platform and dusted each animal, a sense of pride and ownership filling her. Of course she didn't own the ride. It was probably worth thousands of dollars. But it was under her care. When she reached the golden horse, she paused, afraid to approach it.

"It's just a wooden horse," she muttered, forcing herself to take the last step. She wiped it down, not rushing, but careful to avoid looking into its eyes. Then she tallied up the day's sales and recorded them in the log. The total didn't even cover her salary. She supposed the park subsidized the cost.

She locked up and walked to her car. It was a pleasant evening, still light and warm, without the oppressive heat of day. When she saw a man standing by her car, her heart skipped a beat. It was not, however, Gage. It was Ben.

"Hi. What are you doing here?" She was happy to see him and tried to keep any hint of disappointment out of her voice.

"There's a hiking trail in the park. I thought we could take it if you're not too tired."

"Sure. Is this a good excuse to get more pictures?"

"Partly, but I also wanted to talk to you."

Penny sent her sister a text, telling her she'd be home late. "Lead the way."

They passed by the governor's house to get to the trail. "You feel anything here?"

"No, but I might if I went inside."

"I should have asked how long the trail was before agreeing to walk it."

"It's only about two miles, but it's rated moderate."

Penny wasn't really worried about the difficulty. Waitressing kept her in shape, as did walking to and from work. Of course, she wouldn't be doing that anymore. She needed to step up her hunt for a new car.

They walked for a while fast enough to get Penny's heart rate up. She reduced her speed enough to talk. "Did you fix things with Juniper?"

"Yeah. We're okay. If I wanted a shot with her, I should have gone for it."

"You can't expect her to wait forever."

"Exactly. I was acting like Adam stole my favorite toy, but she put me straight."

"Can we pause for a moment? I guess I'm not in as good of shape as I thought."

"Sure, I want to get some pictures, anyway."

Penny leaned against a tree and sucked air into her lungs. Ben was also breathing heavily, but he puttered about snapping pictures.

"She berated me for letting you go."

Penny had not thought Juniper approved of her dating Ben, but that was before Adam entered the picture. "Did she want you to kidnap me and lock me in the basement? The breakup was mutual and the right thing to do if you're hung up on Juniper."

"I'm not. I admit it really bothered me at first, her dating someone else, especially someone I considered superficial and bound to hurt her. But there's a reason I chose you over her."

"The thrill of the chase?" Penny kept her tone light. When their relationship ended, it hurt, but Ben hadn't broken her heart. She had yet to truly give her heart to anyone. She wasn't sure she would ever trust another person enough to make her that vulnerable.

"Hilarious. You're beautiful, inside and out. You have a spark about you, perhaps because of your psychic gift."

Penny pushed away from the tree and continued down the path. Her cheeks heated, and she couldn't meet Ben's gaze. "I'm kind of seeing someone else."

"Gage?"

Penny stopped. "How did you know?"

"I always sensed something between the two of you."

"It's early days yet, and my new job hasn't helped matters, but we're trying."

"It's all right. If we're being honest, things weren't working out with us." Ben held out his hand and after a brief hesitation, Penny took it. They walked in silence for a few more minutes, but it wasn't uncomfortable.

"I didn't know the park was so big."

"The land must be worth a fortune. The county was lucky someone donated it."

"Stand over there. I want to get your picture. I've been selling some of my photos online. If this turns out well, will you sign a release?"

"Sure." She walked over to the edge of the trail. Now that she knew the image might appear on a stock photo site, she didn't know what to do with her hands and suspected her smile looked forced and cheesy. The ground dropped off away from the path, heading down towards the Missouri River.

"Stay there. I want to get another angle." Leaves from the previous fall crackled underfoot as he left the trail, looking for the perfect spot. "Maybe I should climb this tree."

"No tree climbing. You'll fall out and break something."

"Challenge accepted." Ben tucked his camera into its carrying case, hopped on a low-lying branch and hauled himself up to a mid-level branch.

"I'm serious. You're going to get hurt." Having not quite grown into his long legs and oversized feet, Ben sometimes tripped walking across the floor. He had no business leaving the ground.

He inched out on the edge of the branch, testing its strength. "The sacrifices I make for my art." Holding onto the branch with one hand, he fumbled for his camera with the other.

A loud bang echoed through the woods. Penny felt a burning pain tear through her arm. She screamed and lost her balance, falling off the edge. When she hit the ground, the pain exploded, and she barely noticed herself tumbling down the hill. She couldn't focus on anything but the fire in her arm. She bounced a few more times, each jolt ratcheting up the burn.

After what seemed like forever, she ground to a halt, cradled in a dip on the hillside. She curled into a fetal position, grabbing her arm. Her fingers grew sticky with blood, and the coppery scent filled her nostrils. Had someone shot her?

Paralyzed by pain and fear, she couldn't move. She whimpered and then tried again. "Ben!"

Another gunshot.

Penny cut her scream short. Had the sniper shot Ben? Was he wounded? Dead? She couldn't go there. Breath hissed in and out of her lungs. Was the sniper even now searching for survivors? Would he track her down and finish the job?

She was going to hyperventilate. She forced herself to breathe more slowly. Gritting her teeth against the pain, she made it to her knees, her left hand still clasped tightly against her right arm. "Ben." This time, she whispered.

"Penny, thank God." Ben was also keeping his voice low.

A stick broke, and Penny's breath froze. Ben or the unknown assailant? Using her one good arm, she tried to push herself to her feet, but her vision blurred around the edges and she sunk back to her knees.

A scuffling sound preceded Ben's arrival. Red scratches stood out on his pale face, but Penny saw no other blood.

"Someone is shooting at us. I thought you were dead."

"Likewise." Penny swayed and Ben stumbled the last few feet towards her, catching her up in his arms. Penny cried out and grew limp.

Chapter 13

P enny had fainted. Ben laid her gently on the ground, noticing for
the first time the blood streaming down her arm. He pried her
hand away from the wound. An ugly gash showed where the bullet had
torn through her arm. He guessed it hurt like hell, but didn't think it
was a life-threatening injury.

He tried to tear his tee shirt, but he had fallen out of the tree at the
sound of the gun and landed on his wrist. It had already doubled in
size, and there was no way he could use it. He pulled his shirt over his
head and, using his elbow to stabilize the fabric, tied it in a makeshift
bandage around Penny's arm. She stirred and opened her eyes.

"We have to get out of here. I don't know if he'll come after us, but
we can't take the chance," he said.

She nodded, face grim. "Can you help me up?"

"I'd carry you, but I think I broke my wrist falling out of that tree."

"Told you so."

There was nothing funny about their situation, but Ben was glad
to hear the hint of humor. He slid his good arm under hers and got
her on her feet. "We should call for help, but can you climb the hill? It
would make it easier for paramedics to find us." It would also make it
easier for the sniper to try again.

It took them a long time to reach the top of the hill. He half dragged Penny the last few feet. When they reached the trail, they collapsed into a heap, both panting.

"I guess it's no longer a question that someone sabotaged my car."

"Who would want you dead?"

"Ron has contacts in and out of prison. He could have hired someone. Or it could be Archie Jenkins."

"The job's not worth killing someone." He didn't even understand why Penny had given up her job at the Carriage House Cafe to run the carousel. The hours were shorter, but the commute was longer, and she would soon have the added expense of another car.

"It's not just the job. He thinks I suckered his father into offering me the job, taking something rightfully his. He may even think his father wrote me into his will."

"Did he?"

"Write me into his will? I doubt it. Doubt he even had many assets to give away. But if he thinks I tried to take his place in his father's affections... I don't know."

"It's weak, but I've heard worse motives for murder." Disgruntled employees sometimes brought a gun into work, ready to wreak vengeance on those they blamed for their own failings. Sometimes they might even have real grievances, not that it justified their actions.

Penny shivered, despite the warm air, and Ben worried she might go into shock. He pulled out his phone, thankful when he saw he had a signal. They weren't far from civilization, it just felt like they were.

He placed the call to 911. The dispatcher kept him on the phone after she sent police and an ambulance to their location.

"Is the shooter still there?"

"I don't think so. We haven't heard any more shots."

"You're both injured?"

"My friend got shot in the arm. I broke my wrist."

"Help will be there soon. Stay on the line."

"Okay." Ben drew Penny in close to warm her with his body heat. He heard sirens, but knew it would still be awhile before the paramedics arrived since they would have to come in on foot. He was feeling chilly himself without a shirt. The sun dipped below the horizon and the shadows were lengthening. The sniper would have heard the sirens, too, and should be well away by now. He hoped.

The police reached them first. The officer drew his pistol and scanned the area for the sniper. A few minutes later, the medics arrived carrying a stretcher. They put Penny on the stretcher and gave Ben a blanket to wrap around his shoulders. Then they all began the long trek out.

The police officer holstered his gun, but remained vigilant. Ben's fear eased when they exited the trail, but he didn't relax until they reached the parking lot. The paramedics hoisted the stretcher into the ambulance, and Ben followed. With the shriek of the siren, they were on their way to the hospital.

Upon arrival, they took Ben for an x-ray and Penny to an exam room. Ben waited for what seemed like a long time, but finally the films came back, confirming the break.

A nurse brought him the bad news and a fresh shirt, since Penny still had his blood-soaked tee. Ben took the shirt but placed it in his lap, unsure if he could wrestle it over his head. His wrist throbbed like crazy. "Thanks."

"You get to pick your cast color."

"Even adults, huh?"

"Why not? Here, let me help you with that."

Ben welcomed the assistance, and the nurse eased the scrub top over his head.

"I heard you were quite the hero."

"I wouldn't say that. I just fell out of a tree and broke my wrist."

"But you stayed to help your friend even though people were shooting at you."

Ben allowed the woman to fuss over him. It felt good to be seen as heroic rather than clumsy. Shock was wearing off, and he was only now realizing how close they had come to death.

The doctor came in and applied the bright blue plaster Ben had chosen. Afterwards, the nurse let him into the waiting room, where the police officer waited to grill him about what had happened.

"You didn't see your attacker?"

"No. I heard the shot, saw Penny fall, and panicked. I fell out of the tree and raced to the trail's edge. As I stood there, trying to find Penny, the gunman fired another shot. I threw myself to the ground and crawled down the hill. You saw how dense the brush is. It took me a while to find her."

"Do you think Penny was his target?"

"I don't know. She recently started a new job and the man who thought he should get it has been hassling her."

The police officer asked for the man's name and any more information Ben had on him.

"I only know he's the son of the man who used to operate the park carousel."

The officer took Ben's contact details and left him alone in the waiting room. When the doctor finished stitching Penny's arm, the officer questioned her.

Her story matched Ben's. She'd been posing for a picture when she heard a loud noise, felt pain in her arm, and fell down the hill. Too weak to move, she'd stayed where she landed until Ben found her and helped her back to the trail. She had also heard a second shot and feared for Ben.

"I'll be in touch if I have any more questions for you," the police officer said. "We don't get many shootings in this neighborhood. Officers are canvassing the scene, trying to determine where the shooter fired the shots. Then they will search that area for clues. In the meantime, I'll check out Archie Jenkins. But if this was a random shooting, it will be difficult to solve."

"What about Ron?" Ben whispered, drawing the officer's attention.

"If you have any more information, you need to share it with me."

Penny bit her lip. "A couple months ago, a man named Ron kidnapped Ben. Some friends and I helped rescue him, and Ron went to prison. He holds a grudge against us, but as far as I know, he's still behind bars."

"Ron seems to have more of a motive than this Archie guy, but he also has an alibi."

"He could have hired someone," Ben said.

The officer's eyes narrowed, but he didn't deny the possibility. "I'll look into Ron, too." He tucked his notepad away.

"How are we going to get home?" Ben asked. "Our cars are at the park."

"I can give you a ride."

When the policeman dropped them off back at the park, Penny said. "I can't drive for a few weeks with this arm. And they gave me something for pain, so I probably shouldn't drive, anyway."

Ben waved his cast at her. "I'm not supposed to drive either, but I can get us home. What are you going to do tomorrow? Call in sick?"

"I can't. This is my first week as the permanent caretaker."

"Someone shot you. I think that's a valid excuse for missing a day of work."

"Maybe," Penny mumbled, but Ben got the feeling she didn't agree.

He drove her home and insisted on coming in with her. When Dora saw his cast and the thick bandage around Penny's arm, she demanded to know what had happened.

Penny collapsed on the couch. "I'm not up to going over it again. You tell her."

Ben explained how they went for a hike and someone had shot at them. "The bullet grazed Penny's arm, and I fell and broke my wrist, but we're both okay. The hospital didn't even want to keep Penny overnight."

"She has a gunshot wound," Dora said in disbelief.

"The bullet didn't hit any major organs. The doctors expect me to make a full recovery, although it's possible I'll have some muscle damage."

Ben scowled. She hadn't mentioned that to him. "See that your sister takes off work tomorrow. It's been quite a day. I need to get going or I'll be crashing on your couch."

"You're welcome to stay," Dora offered.

Penny agreed. "You saved my life. The least I can do is offer you the use of my couch."

"If it wasn't for me, you wouldn't have been on the trail."

"If it wasn't for her obsession with the carousel, she would have been safe at the cafe," Dora argued. "You won't be able to work for a few days. I think you should quit. Or maybe they'll fire you."

Ben didn't miss the venomous look Penny sent her sister. He didn't have the energy to deal with a sibling squabble and didn't want to spend the night on their couch. He was going to have enough trouble sleeping with the pain in his wrist. And with only one good hand, he might have to cancel some client appointments.

"Thanks for the offer, ladies, but I need to get home and take some pain reliever."

Despite the dark circles under her eyes and her stilted movements, Penny walked him to the door. "Looks like this time I'm bringing you into danger." Penny had dragged her feet on the other paranormal cases they had worked, not really wanting to get involved.

"Let's call it even."

"I meant what I said about you saving my life. Not just because you called for help and got us out of there." Her green eyes held his for a moment. "If you hadn't been waiting for me when I got off work, he might have been."

Chapter 14

Dora helped Penny get ready for bed. Penny knew by the pinched expression on her sister's face that Dora was still angry with her. Dora didn't understand the sense of satisfaction Penny got from taking care of the old carousel. Penny wasn't sure she understood it herself. Was it simply the historical value? Penny had an affinity for old things like the house they rented and the house where they had lived with their grandmother. One reason she'd applied at the Carriage House Cafe was because the architecture charmed her and she had been intrigued by how Gage had turned an old stable building into a trendy restaurant.

But if she was to be honest, she knew it was more than the historical significance of the ride. Without the golden horse, the carousel would be only an interesting novelty. Getting the splinter connected her to the brilliantly carved horse. It was still a block of wood. Yet it was more, just like the dolls Juniper had told them about. Unlike the dolls, however, Penny didn't think the spirit or entity haunting it was evil.

"I won't be able to hear you if you call out once I remove my hearing aid for bed," Dora said. "I wish Ben would have stayed."

"I'll be fine. With his broken wrist, he wouldn't be comfortable on the couch."

"I can't believe you're okay with this. Usually Ben drags you into his investigations. This time you're jumping in with both feet, quitting your job, and putting yourself and the rest of us in danger."

Ah. Dora was not just worried about her sister, but about herself as well. "I'm sorry about the car crash. It must have been very traumatic for you. I didn't know at the time that Archie was anything more than a nuisance. I told the police I suspect he was the shooter. They're going to investigate him and hopefully put him behind bars."

"And if they don't find any evidence against him?"

"I'll be on my guard now that I know what he's capable of. And the police will watch him even if they can't arrest him." She didn't mention they were also going to look into Ron. No point in giving Dora something else to worry about. Besides, she was sure Archie was behind her car troubles and the shooting.

Even with the painkillers the doctors had given her, her arm burned like fire. She stayed strong for her sister, but once Dora left her alone, she sank down on her pillows, clutching her arm with a whimper. It was almost impossible to find a comfortable position to sleep in.

Finally, however, her exhaustion and the drugs in her system overcame the discomfort, and she slipped into a troubled slumber. Dreams skittered through her mind. Dreams of being chased, hunted, shot at. This time, when the bullet hit her, she fell off a cliff rather than down a hill. She tumbled for what seemed like forever, the ground rushing up to meet her. She awoke with a start before she hit, her heart pounding.

She was thirsty enough to make the painful trip downstairs to the kitchen, where she poured herself a glass of water. She didn't see Plato anywhere and guessed he was sleeping with Dora. Her arm hurt and she hadn't yet picked up the prescription the doctor had given her, so she swallowed some ibuprofen. Not wanting to make this trip again, she brought the bottle and a glass of orange juice upstairs with her.

To her surprise, she fell back asleep almost immediately, and the dreams rushed in.

It was dark except for the bonfire burning at the base of the tree. Not close enough to cause harm, of course, for the tree was sacred. Ancient, too. She couldn't wrap her arms fully around the trunk. All the trees in the grove were special, but the largest among them was the mother. The giver of life.

There were other people around, but everyone was quiet until their spiritual leader spoke. He prayed to the mother goddess, and the crowd repeated his words. They formed hands around the bonfire and danced. The words swelled to a chant, spoken every year on this day for centuries. Perhaps longer.

Times were good, and the goddess wanted only their fidelity and praise. Crops and people would prove fruitful. Peace would continue if they kept to their uneasy alliances. They raised their voices to the branches overhead and the stars beyond. All was well and would continue to be so if they gave their goddess her due. The fire crackled and burned.

When Penny's alarm went off the next morning, she groggily dragged herself through layers of sleep. She turned the beeping off and sat on the edge of her bed, feeling exhausted. She needed to pick up her prescription before going to work, or she would never make it through the day.

She used the dregs of the orange juice to swallow a couple more ibuprofen tablets. Since Ben had a broken wrist, in part because of her, she called Gage and asked him for a ride. If he couldn't do it, she would get a rideshare. Her car was still at the park and she hoped she would feel well enough to drive home, despite doctor's orders.

She placed the call to Gage, and as the phone rang, a faint memory tugged at her consciousness. There was something about music. Some kind of singing. She reached for the memory, but it disintegrated like cotton candy. Was it a dream? She vaguely recalled nightmares about being shot and falling off a cliff. Had there been singing? Why would she sing as she tumbled to her death?

"Hello," Gage answered.

"Hey, it's Penny. I need a favor." Penny would need all her persuasion skills to convince him to take her to work. Like Dora, he would try to convince her to stay home. But she wasn't her father's daughter for nothing. When she wanted, she could turn on the charm.

"Fine. I'll come get you. But I think you're making a mistake."

"Thanks, I really appreciate it." It wouldn't be the first time she'd made a mistake, but hopefully it wouldn't have the horrible consequences of not foreseeing Dora's accident. She didn't see how it could, since it only affected her. When she read for others, she was careful to emphasize that their actions determined the future, not the cards. The cards were only a tool.

A tool she had not consulted when deciding whether to take the carousel job.

***

"I've always given you time off for electric shocks, burns, and near-death experiences," Gage reminded her. "Your new boss is less accommodating."

"You're a good employer. I never meant to imply otherwise. But I like this job and thought things might be less confusing if I wasn't working for you any longer." Penny dug the fingernails of her left hand into her palm. What if she'd totally misunderstood what was going on between her and Gage?

Gage gave her a quick glance before turning his attention back to the road. "Do you feel I am sexually harassing you?"

"No, of course not. But if things end badly, we're stuck working with each other."

"Do you expect things to end badly?"

"I don't think anyone ever starts dating someone if they think it will end badly." She shuffled her feet. Her arm hurt despite her having picked up and taken her prescription. Why was Gage giving her a hard time? He had to know she wasn't at her best.

"If we break up, I won't take it out on you at work."

Penny sighed. "No, I don't think you would, but things would still be awkward. I've only just started feeling comfortable with Ben."

"Comfortable enough for him to meet you after work."

There was an edge to Gage's voice. Was he jealous? "We went for a hike. As friends."

"And nearly both got killed. I checked Ron's status. He's still in prison, so if he's behind the attack, he must have hired someone."

"It's Archie Jenkins. He thinks the carousel job should have been his."

"Then let him have it. If you don't want to work for the cafe anymore, you can get another job. Lots of places are hiring and I'll give you a glowing recommendation."

"Elliot, the older Mr. Jenkins, entrusted the job to me. I don't want to let him down."

Gage muttered something under his breath as he turned into the parking lot. Penny ignored him. Although she knew she was in for a grueling day with her sore arm in a sling, a sense of peace filled her at the sight of the carousel building. This was where she belonged. In her bag, underneath the lunch she'd packed from home, was Ben's shirt, crusted with her blood. She wasn't sure what she was going to do with it, but had obeyed the compulsion to bring it along.

"Thanks for the ride. I'll see you later."

Gage frowned, his brows dipping towards his nose. His blue eyes were chilly. "Call if you need a ride home. You're going to be tired after working all day and you're not supposed to drive."

Penny nodded and closed the car door behind her. She dug out her keycard as she neared the entrance. To her surprise, the door was unlocked. She paused. She was sure she had locked it yesterday. Had someone broken in? Should she ask Gage to come in with her? He might not have left yet.

Taking a deep breath, she pushed the door open. She half expected to see the beautiful carousel vandalized, graffiti sprayed on the walls, paint thrown over the animals, trash and beer cans littering the platform. To her relief, it appeared untouched. She released the air in her lungs in a rush.

Her supervisor was there, however, and marched over to greet Penny. "We didn't expect you to be in today after what happened yesterday."

"You heard about that?"

"Of course. The police informed the park department right away. It's very unusual for us to have a shooting."

"I didn't want to take time off since I'm still so new to the job. I'll keep my arm protected." She nodded to her sling. "I'm sure I can manage."

Her supervisor looked uncomfortable. "I'm afraid there is another problem."

Penny stiffened. "What's wrong?"

"Come and sit down." The woman led her to a bench by the carousel. "The park department received an anonymous tip."

"About the shooting?"

"No. About you."

A chill snaked down Penny's spine. "What about me?"

"I know it was a long time ago, but we can't have someone with a criminal record working the carousel. There are children here. I'm sure you understand."

"I don't have a criminal record."

"Not officially. You were a juvenile, so the records are sealed. But the police arrested you."

Penny's hand trembled. She took a deep breath. "If my records are sealed, how did you get them?"

"Like I said, someone passed the information on to our office. I don't think we have the actual records, just a newspaper account of the incident."

Penny closed her eyes, thrown back to that moment of time. Her father pressuring her to wear short skirts and low-cut blouses. High heels setting fire to her feet. Hanging around bars, nursing a watered down soda, since she wasn't old enough to drink and tossing around her red hair. The places all served food, so it wasn't illegal for her to be there, so long as she didn't drink, but she suspected her father slipped the bartender a little something extra for his trouble.

It never took long for a man to approach her. A few bats of her mascaraed eyelashes was usually enough to convince him to play pool with her. A little money on the outcome, just for fun.

What the poor marks didn't know was the hours she had spent practicing under the watchful eyes of her father. He was deadly with a pool cue and often played the role of pool shark himself, but found it was much easier for his pretty daughter to drum up business.

But they overplayed their hand. Her youth and bright hair made her stand out. Local precincts received complaints, and eventually she batted her eyes at an undercover cop.

The police charged her with gambling. The case never even made it to court. She plea bargained to a lesser charge and did some community service. She spent one night in jail. It had taken that long for her dad to bail her out. It had been enough, however. The horror of being locked in a cage left its mark. From then on she had refused to have anything to do with her father's schemes. She'd thought it only a footnote in her past, a footnote buried so deep no one would ever notice it.

She had forgotten about the newspaper article, although calling it an article was a stretch. A bar patron had snapped pictures of her being arrested. Penny would never forget the police officer yanking her arms behind her back and snapping cold, harsh cuffs on her wrists. In the photos she looked less like the femme fatale her father had groomed and more like a child playing with her mother's makeup. The picture, along with a few paragraphs explaining how she had "hoodwinked" honest citizens out of their hard-earned money, had appeared in a local suburban journal. Most suburban journals had folded years ago. How had someone even found a copy to send to the park department? But she was sure she knew who was responsible. It seemed Archie was good at more than tinkering with cars and taking potshots.

"They seal juvenile records for a reason, giving young people a second chance."

"Which is why we would like you to resign. We don't want to make a big deal about it and we'll provide you with a clean reference."

"They charged me with gambling. Have you ever played poker with your friends or joined a football pool? Technically, that's illegal, although you can go to the casino and gamble all you want without penalty."

The woman's face hardened, her eyes becoming less sympathetic. "Don't make this harder than it has to be. The park department is even willing to give you two weeks' severance money."

What could she do? It would be useless to fight them. If they made the article common knowledge, she might not get a job anywhere. Rage simmered beneath her fear. First, Archie had tried to kill her. Twice, if she counted the sabotaged brakes. Since that failed, he was trying to ruin her life.

Her dad had put her in this position, making her vulnerable when he should have been protecting her. She had forgiven him just a few short months ago for her chaotic childhood, but she realized now that forgiveness wasn't one and done. It was an ongoing process, one she didn't feel capable of tackling today. Today she would be angry. At Archie, the park department and her dad.

"I see. So what do I do now? Go home?"

"Go home, take care of your injury. Since you signed up for automatic deposit, we will send your severance package directly to your bank account. I only need you to sign this paper."

Penny stared blankly at the sheet of paper the woman handed her. The words blurred before her, but said something about deciding she really needed full-time hours and a job closer to home. She took the pen and signed her name.

She thrust the paper back at her supervisor. Did they really think she would hurt children or be a destructive influence on them? Or did this have more to do with her attack on park grounds? She hadn't intended to sue, but certainly couldn't do so now with the leverage the park had over her.

She stood, pulled off her park vest and dropped it on the bench. Her chest constricted, forcing the air out of her lungs. What could she do? Drive home, first. A twinge of pain shot down her arm at the thought, but she gritted her teeth. She could do it. She certainly wouldn't ask the park department, or anyone else, for help.

She felt as if she was walking through water, not air, as she trudged towards the door. Her shoulder blades twitched with the sensation of being watched. By the supervisor, maybe, but definitely by the golden horse. Could she see out of her painted eyes? Or did she just know her caretaker was leaving her? Penny felt the pull, the compulsion, to turn back and throw herself on the mercy of the supervisor. To beg for her job back. To throw her arms around the living, yet inanimate, horse and refuse to leave. But she resisted, taking one step after another until she finally reached the door and crossed the threshold.

The muggy warmth of the June morning hit her square in the face. Though temperatures were still bearable, it looked to be a hot day. A day when mothers, picnicking and playing with their children on the playground, might be happy to spend a few dollars, escape the heat for a while and give their children a treat. She predicted a busy day for the carousel, although she wouldn't be there to see it.

She didn't make it to her car. Gage was still there, waiting.

"Did you change your mind about staying? I can take you home and bring Dora out later today so she can pick up the car."

"The park department knew about the shooting. Didn't expect me to come in."

"That makes sense. So they already have someone to cover for you?"

Penny chuckled without humor. "Yes, permanently. I'm fired."

"What? They can't do that. You're hurt. Someone shot you on their property."

"After hours."

Gage waved that aside. "Still wouldn't look good for them if this gets out."

"It won't get out." Penny fought to keep her face expressionless as Gage studied her.

"What's wrong? Why would they treat you like this?"

"I'll take you up on the ride. I think I overestimated my strength."

"Of course. I shouldn't have kept you standing here while I interrogated you." Gage helped her to his car, opened the door for her, and even buckled her seatbelt. "I remember how much a gunshot hurts."

Ron had shot him during their showdown on the Sunflower. "Your injury was far worse." Gage had required surgery to fix his shoulder while the hospital had treated and released Penny.

"Yes, but I wasn't running around the day after I got shot trying to prove I could still handle everything." He started the car and waited until they exited the park to speak again. "You're not going to fight for wrongful termination?"

"No, I quit."

"I thought you said they fired you."

"Technically, I quit." She blinked her eyes against the weight of tears. She might as well tell him. He would find out eventually. "They blackmailed me."

There was a long silence. "I'm confused. Why would they do that? And what would..."

"What would they have against me? That's the million dollar question, right? You already know my dad's in jail."

Gage nodded.

"I neglected to mention, I got in some trouble with pool hustling. I never cheated, but I purposely misled people into betting against me. The cops charged me with gambling, but the case never actually went to court."

"Gambling? You never even played the slots when we went to Ron's casino. I didn't think you were a fan."

"I'm not. At least not anymore."

"Besides, I didn't think the police cared about small-time gambling."

"They made an exception for me."

Gage pulled onto the highway and merged into traffic. "I checked your record before hiring you. Nothing came up."

"My record's clean. I was a juvenile, so my records are sealed, and it never went to trial."

"Then how did they find out?"

"Archie. He dug up an old newspaper article."

"What's going on? This man tampered with your car, shot at you and Ben, and is now smearing your reputation. All to get a part-time park job? It doesn't make sense."

"It's a family tradition. His father made a career out of running the carousel and his grandfather helped carve one of the horses."

"Not an excuse for murder."

"I'm not going to worry about it anymore. It's over and my arm hurts." Her arm burned, but no way was it over. She would have to get back to the carousel, maybe just as a frequent rider. She could still feel its tug, like she was a fish on the end of a line.

"Come back to the cafe after your arm heals. We are still within the two-week window."

Penny had planned to return to the cafe after Mr. Jenkins recovered, but the supervisor's words left her feeling inadequate. "Aren't you afraid I will corrupt any children that come in with their parents?"

"That was their excuse?"

"Can you blame them? I'm the daughter of a convicted felon with a record of my own."

"You're not responsible for your father's actions and neither of you ever targeted children. How did you get started pool hustling?"

Gage hadn't turned away from her in disgust, but she couldn't read his well-modulated expression. "My dad taught me the game and how to pretend I was a silly airhead. My opponents thought me a simple way to win twenty bucks, but the money ended up in my pocket."

"Your dad set you up."

"He didn't force me."

"You were still a child."

Legally, yes, but Penny hadn't felt like a child for a long time. "I knew what I was doing."

Gage drew up in front of her house. "Did you?" He cupped her chin and tilted her face to his. "Don't worry about the park service. It's their loss. I'll be happy to have you back."

Penny struggled to hold his gaze. "It will be weeks before I can carry a tray."

"Come back when you're ready."

Penny nodded, but didn't think that day would come.

Chapter 15

After dropping Penny off at her house, Gage stopped by the restaurant to check in and then drove out to the agency where he used to work. They owned an office in a nondescript office park filled with an insurance agency, a hair salon, and a tax specialist. Or so it appeared on the surface. For the first time, he wondered if any of the other small businesses were fronts for something else.

The receptionist, Trudy, greeted him with a smile and rang Steve to come get him. The agent arrived within a few minutes.

"I didn't expect to see you today."

"Impulse visit," Gage said. "Do you have time for a consult?"

"Sure." Steve took him in the back, where people sat in cubicles working on computers. On the main level, the employees were ordinary head hunters. The real magic happened downstairs. The agency was far larger below ground than above.

Before heading below, Steve took Gage to his office, a small space crowded with a desk, overflowing bookshelves, and a guest chair. A window overlooked the parking lot.

"You must be moving up in the world." Gage nodded at the window.

"Got a promotion. Still cramped, though." He sat behind the desk and Gage took the guest chair. "Ready to try one of the more experimental procedures?"

"It's time I give your experimental potion a try." Penny's obsession with the carousel worried Gage, but he was more concerned with Archie Jenkins. If Penny was right in her suspicions, the man would do whatever it took to get what he wanted, even if what he wanted didn't seem to make any sense.

Losing his remote viewing abilities had crushed Gage, but recently he realized he'd lost more than a part of himself. He'd lost a valuable skill he could use to protect those he cared about.

"Great. I just need you to sign some paperwork." Steve left the office, returning with a stack of pages. "Read and sign where indicated. I'll go check with the lab."

Gage skimmed through the material. As he had expected, the agency wanted to remove themselves from any liability. He assumed all risks, which is why he'd been hesitant to sign up in the past, preferring to research on his own. But so far his research had provided little but dead ends.

"Ready?" Steve asked.

Gage handed over the papers and followed Steve down to the lab. The agency combined the knowledge of scientists and magic workers to make various potions designed to enhance psychic ability. It was all experimental and unpleasant side effects were common. So far no one had ever died from the prototypes, but Gage had initialed a page in the release forms, acknowledging the possibility.

Steve removed a vial from a refrigerator and poured a green liquid into a cup. "Drink this and then go lie down in that room." He pointed towards a dark room with a couch. "You should fall asleep. When you wake up, we'll run some tests."

Gage raised the glass, the liquid sloshing against the rim from the faint tremor in his hand. He sniffed it. "Smells like watermelon."

"Probably artificial to make it taste better. You don't have to do this. The cafe is doing well, right? And you have your investments."

"It's not because I need the money. If you lost your skills, wouldn't you want to regain them?"

"I don't have any psychic ability."

"Maybe not, but you've got skills which make you valuable to the agency. Don't tell me you'd be content to take a job topside filing resumes."

Steve shook his head. "There are other places to work."

"I know, but wish me luck." Gage raised his glass to his friend and downed the liquid in one go. The watermelon taste was strong, but couldn't disguise the bitterness underneath. Fuzziness crept over his brain almost immediately. He stumbled on his way to the room, barely making it to the couch before his legs stopped working. He half fell onto the couch, struggled to pull his legs up, and drifted into an uneasy sleep. A distant part of him wondered if this was how it felt to Penny when restless spirits shared their lives with her through her dreams.

He drifted into the sky, floating above the earth. Beneath him, he could see a lush countryside, crisscrossed by roads and bisected by a river curving through the center. Mountains rose on one end, their peaks capped with snow. He drifted higher, above fluffy looking clouds. He reached out and touched one, but it felt cold and wet and his hand passed right through. The clouds obscured the landscape below, the green fading, the mountains vanishing, until he could only see a faint swirl of the river.

Then came the noise. He tried to raise his hands to block his ears, but his body remained frozen on the couch while he drifted weightless in the sky. The discordant sounds bashed around in his head, screeching like fingernails on a chalkboard and banging like cymbals. He couldn't think, couldn't escape the cacophony. Fear flickered at the edge of his consciousness. Would the drug leave him deaf, like Dora?

With one last clang, the noise faded. His ears rang, but he welcomed the silence even as he drifted higher. It was cold in the upper reaches of the atmosphere. It struck first at his hands and feet. He longed to flex his aching hands, but couldn't move. He lay helpless as the cold slid up his limbs and pooled in the center of his body. Surely the leaden weight in his body would drag him down, stop his ascent, perhaps send him plummeting back to earth.

But no, he drifted upward. As he grew closer to the sun, which he could now see growing ever larger in his peripheral vision, the cold fled. He grew warm and then hot. Sweat trickled down his back. The fear flickered back, stronger. Would the sun incinerate him?

He smelled smoke. Was the lab burning down around him? The sun grew larger, the trickle of sweat became a torrent. He drew in a lungful of smoky air, coughing. There was an alcoholic burn to the smoke, and he suddenly felt as if someone had doused him with perfume. Floral, woodsy, and spicy scents assaulted his nostrils. Their pleasant aroma masked the smoke, but made his nose burn. As the various scents warred for dominance, his stomach lurched and he worried he might be sick.

Just in time, the smells dissipated. The heat, too. He drifted peacefully, cocooned in a cloud of feathery softness, not the cold wetness he had touched earlier. He sank into the downy luxury. It was quiet. There were no extremes of temperature or battery of scents and sounds. He glimpsed the distant stars before they, too, disappeared and darkness descended.

***

Penny typed the last words of her email reading for Jackson. He had taken her advice and approached Micah, the lead singer of Hyperbolic, with some of his ideas. There had been resistance at first, but when he'd threatened to walk out, Micah listened.

Penny re-read the message Jackson had sent her.

Jackson: **He warned me not to get full of myself. Drummers are more replaceable than singers. But he's giving me the chance to write our next song. If he likes it, we'll record it.**

Penny's heart rate sped up, and her chest grew warm. It felt good to help people, and she believed Jackson was going places, with or without Hyperbolic. She hoped he stayed with the group. He didn't want to leave, and she suspected the already popular group could reach new heights with his contribution. But that would depend, in part, on Micah and his willingness to share the spotlight.

Her phone chimed as she was putting her tarot cards away. She had a text from the cafe, but it didn't come from Gage. Instead, the cook was asking if she could come in.

Marjory: **Gage said you were back on the payroll. He's out sick and I was hoping you could come in and run things. I know you're injured, but you won't have to wait tables.**

Gage was out sick? The only other times he had missed work was when Ron shot him and when he'd nearly gotten blown up by a bomb. He'd seemed fine when he brought her home yesterday. It must be a fast-acting and heavy-hitting virus.

Penny: **I'll be in soon.**

Plato sat by her feet. "Sorry, buddy. I've got to work." She could have sworn the dog frowned at her. "I know I promised you a walk, but the cafe will fall apart without at least me or Gage there."

He looked so soulfully at her, however, that she hooked him up to his leash and brought him to the restaurant with her. She would sneak him into Gage's office. So long as he stayed out of the kitchen and dining area, no one would even know he was there.

After settling Plato in the office with a chew toy and throw pillow, Penny entered the kitchen. Marjory had already assigned jobs based on who was available. Penny saw no reason to make changes. "I'll be in Gage's office if you need me. If it gets busy, I can manage the register, but I can't do any tables."

"How's your arm?" Marjory asked.

"Like I got stung by a gigantic bee. Did Gage say what was wrong with him?"

"I didn't talk to him. He just sent a text saying he was sick and wouldn't be in today."

"That's odd." Although he didn't micromanage, Gage kept a close eye on the cafe.

"He's the boss. What's the use of owning the place if you can't play hooky now and then."

"So you don't think he's really sick?"

"I'll deny it if you tell him, but I think he needed a break. He's been crabby."

Back in Gage's office, Penny worked on the schedule for next week. She couldn't help but feel guilty. If Gage had been irritable, it was probably because he had been doing her work besides his own. Now that she was back on familiar ground, she couldn't quite remember why it had seemed so important to take the carousel job. Fewer and more regular hours had been attractive, and she'd wanted to avoid any complications that came from dating her boss, but she could look for other options closer to home. Or maybe it didn't matter that they worked together. Gage wasn't the type to take advantage.

During the lunch rush, she worked the register. A few people asked how she'd hurt her arm and she told them she'd injured it while hiking.

Not a lie, but not the whole truth. Saying someone had shot her would cause needless worry and might hurt the reputation of the cafe if they thought her injury occurred at work. Now that Archie had what he wanted, she didn't think he'd be out to hurt anyone else. And even though she was angry with the park department for her wrongful termination, she didn't want revenge or to damage their reputation. Reputation was a fragile thing, all too easily destroyed by a casual comment or newspaper clipping.

Once business slowed, she took her own lunch, and Plato, out back. There were a handful of tables in front of the cafe for customers, but behind the restaurant they had a picnic table for employees. Penny had ordered a soup and sandwich combo. She dipped a hunk of bread in the soup, savoring it before cutting the sandwich into pieces and placing the plate on the ground for Plato.

"Lucky dog." She watched him wolf down the treat. Although he got more leftovers than the vet would approve, her cooking didn't stack up to that of the cafe. She wasn't a terrible cook, but Marjory outshone her.

From her position she could see the backyard of Sycamore House, the bed-and-breakfast where she had delivered food to on Mother's Day, the day she had first encountered the carousel. So much had happened since then. Brooke had delivered her baby, a sweet little boy, and Penny had gotten mixed up with the Jenkins' family, changed jobs, and survived a car accident and a shooting. Could she really put it all behind her and walk away from the carousel as if she'd never dreamed about it, never given it her blood?

The pull she'd buried in work surged to life. When she lifted her face to the sun, she felt its warmth caress her brow. The breeze tugged at her mane of red hair, scraped back into a ponytail. Penny suddenly felt the urge to take it down, shake it loose, and run through the yard, Plato at her heels. She wanted to be free, like the wild horses in her dreams.

Time to get back to work. The only way she could return to the carousel was as a paying guest, and Penny couldn't imagine riding it under Archie's watchful eyes. Concentrating on the cafe and her tarot business kept the longing under control. She needed to bury herself in work until her desire to throw everything else away for the addictive allure of the carousel faded. Part of her suspected the connection between her and the carousel was blood magic. But another part of her simply didn't understand why she couldn't seem to let it go.

It wasn't like she didn't have other important things in her life. She and Gage were in the heady early days of their relationship, and she wanted things to work out between them. And Dora had been her top priority ever since their mother abandoned them. How had she let the carousel come between her and her sister for even a moment, much less the whole last month?

She carried her dishes inside and stacked them in the sink. She filled a bowl with water and brought it out to Plato.

"Do you want to stay out here or come back to the office? You'll have to be on your best behavior if you come inside."

The dog cocked his head to the side, one ear up and the other flopped down. Then he stood, ready to follow her inside.

"Smart doggy." Penny brought the water bowl in and set in down in a corner of the office. She refilled her soda and moved some of Gage's papers so she could put it on the desk. As she did so, a bright green sticky note caught her eye. Gage had written Steve's name on it, along with a long, scientific looking word, followed by a string of numbers and a question mark. He had attached the note to a stapled paper packet. What did it mean?

Penny knew she shouldn't snoop. This was Gage's office, papers, and research. He couldn't talk much about his time with the agency, but Penny had heard the raw grief in the little he had shared. His loss was deeply personal to him and he wouldn't want her sticking her nose in where it didn't belong.

But he was out sick when he knew she wasn't there to cover. Could it have something to do with this note?

Penny skimmed the page under the note. It read like a research paper and she barely understood half of it, but it appeared to discuss the chemical and arcane properties of an experimental drug, going by the unpronounceable name on the sticky note. She flipped to the next page. It listed warnings and side effects, up to and including—death.

Penny dropped the sheaf of papers. Was this why Gage was out sick? Had he taken this drug? Was he experiencing some sort of dreadful side effect, or worse?

Seeming to sense her distress, Plato left his spot in the corner and nuzzled her. Automatically, Penny reached down to pet him. The dog whined.

"I should go check on him." Penny had never been to Gage's house, but she knew where he lived. She would swing through the restaurant and then walk over. He lived farther away than she did and usually drove to work, but it was doable.

There were only a few customers in the dining room and Marjory appeared to have everything under control in the kitchen.

"I'm going to check on Gage," Penny said.

Marjory raised her brows. "Is that a good idea? You know how he gets."

"I'll call first." But when her call went straight to voicemail, she hooked Plato up to his leash and set out. Marjory caught her before she reached the street.

"You can take my car." The woman handed Penny her keys.

"Thanks. I'll be careful."

"Yeah, just make sure he hasn't done something stupid."

Was Marjory worried that Gage would harm himself? Penny didn't think he would. Not deliberately, anyway. But he might risk taking an experimental drug if he thought it could give him back his psychic ability.

Penny drove over to Gage's house and knocked on the door. No answer. She peered in through the side pane windows, but saw only an empty hallway.

She knocked again. Dialed his phone once more. Nothing. Tried the door. Locked. What could she do? She didn't have a key and despite her checkered past, didn't know how to pick a lock. She gazed at the doormat under her feet. Would Gage do something so obvious?

She lifted the mat by the corner, but the concrete underneath was bare. A pair of flowerpots sporting carnations sat on either side of the door. She looked under one. Bingo. A spare key.

She snatched it and let herself inside. "Gage." She walked down the hall, her footsteps echoing in the silence. "I thought I'd stop by. Marjory said you were sick." Stairs leading to the second floor stood to her left while a room opened off the hallway to her right. Gage obviously used the room as a den, and books and papers covered the desk, just like his desk at the cafe. His laptop balanced precariously on a stack of books as if he'd set it down in a hurry. Bookshelves lined the back wall, bursting with yet more books and boxes.

She found the kitchen and family room in the back of the house. The coffee table was a jumble of yet more books, mugs and cups, and a couple of remote controls. Compared to the rest of the house, the kitchen was neat. No dirty dishes filled the sink.

She went upstairs. "Gage?" There were three bedrooms. The master, with an attached bath, and two smaller rooms sharing a Jack and Jill styled bath. A quick glance at the spare rooms showed one being used for storage and the other sparsely furnished with a bed and dresser.

Feeling like a stalker, Penny entered the master bedroom. It had the personality the spare room had lacked. Landscape paintings hung on the gray-blue walls and a plush, blue comforter covered the king-sized bed. He had either made the bed this morning or had not slept in it the night before. There were no signs of recent illness—no crumpled up tissues, bottles of over-the-counter cold medicine or cough drops.

There was also no sign of a struggle. It didn't look like Gage was sick, but he appeared to have left of his own volition. Someone could have held a gun to his head. But who? As far as she knew, Archie didn't know about Gage. Of course, if he could find an old newspaper article about her, then he could find out where she worked and who owned the restaurant. But he didn't seem to have a motive to hurt Penny anymore, now that he had what he wanted.

A lamp, paperback book, and a pair of reading glasses lay on Gage's nightstand. A pile of clothes graced one corner of the room, and the bathroom counter was littered with toiletries. Penny ran a finger along the spine of the book. It was a thriller by a popular author, but not one she had read. She tried to imagine Gage sitting in bed, reading for a few minutes before turning off the light. Did he ever have company?

She veered away from the thought. Of course he would have had women here. He was older than she was and had more of a past. But the other nightstand was bare save for a matching lamp. She had no reason to believe he was seeing anyone else but her now.

Gage wasn't home. She had no excuse to snoop further. She hurried back down the stairs and checked the attached garage. No car. Unless he had gone to the doctor, Gage was lying about being sick and had another agenda. He was the boss. He could take off whenever he wanted.

She needed to get back to the cafe and return Marjory's car, but as she locked up and slid the spare key back under the flowerpot, panic poured over her like a wave. Her hands trembled and she could almost taste danger on the tip of her tongue. But the threat was not directed at her this time. Or even Gage, though she still worried about him. The carousel was in danger. And she was still its caretaker, job or no job.

I can't run off with Marjory's car. I'll take it back to the cafe and call a rideshare.

Her chest tightened and her heart beat faster. She didn't have time to waste. She needed to get to the carousel now. Marjory would understand. Or not. Grabbing her phone, she scrolled through her contacts and called the park department before leaving Gage's neighborhood.

"Something's wrong at the carousel. Send someone out," she gasped when the answering service picked up, her voice as breathless as if she were running.

Ignoring traffic laws and the pain in her arm, Penny sped towards the bridge which crossed over into St. Louis county. She hoped the police wouldn't pick her up on radar, for she didn't think she could stop even if they tried to pull her over. She drove as fast as she dared, cymbals crashing in her head. The carousel was at risk. *She* was at risk.

Somehow she evaded the police and didn't cause any harm to herself or others. She tore into the parking lot, the rear of the car fishtailing. She slammed on the brakes and fumbled for the door with her good hand. There were only three other cars in the lot. Hers was not one of them. Dora must have picked it up, or the park department had towed it. She suspected the battered old pickup truck belonged to Archie.

She hurtled towards the building. It was after hours. The door should be locked and her card probably wouldn't work. They would have disabled it.

She tugged on the door handle, but it didn't budge. She banged on the metal surface. Archie must still be in there if his truck was in the lot. Was he cleaning or destroying?

"Archie, let me in." She banged some more, unsure if he could even hear her. She dug through her wallet for her key card. Please let it work.

She swiped it through. The red blinking light held steady. She was no longer in the system. Looking around, she spied a rock. She grabbed it and smashed the door handle. Tugged again. Nothing.

Should she try to smash the card reader? If she broke it, would it disable the lock? She raised the rock, then paused. She wasn't sure how card readers worked, but part of the mechanism had to be electric. The rock fell from her hand as she stared at her palm and the raised burn scar. The red light blinked, mocking her.

Penny placed her hand on the card reader, picturing the wires inside pulsing with electricity. Not unlike the nerves of her body.

"Open."

The door clanked, the light turned green, and she twisted the handle, yanking the door wide. She ran through the vestibule and into the room with the carousel. The lights were out and the music off, but it looked whole and undamaged. Was she losing her mind?

A click echoed through the empty room. She'd been so concerned about the carousel, she hadn't even noticed Archie standing by the supply closet. He'd just closed the door and turned to face her. He held an ax over his shoulder.

"I've been expecting you."

Chapter 16

"Put that down." Penny raised her hands in surrender. "What's going on? You got what you wanted. I'm no longer a threat to you."

"You were never a threat to me."

Penny backpedaled. "Of course not. The carousel job belongs to your family. I'm just a fan."

"Really? Why are you here now? We're closed."

"I just felt..."

"Felt what?" He stepped closer. "An unreasonable urge to come here."

Sort of. "I didn't realize how late it was." She took a step back. He hadn't rushed her. Yet.

"It's infected you, too. I didn't think anyone else could feel it."

Archie also felt the pull? She tried to talk to him as if he were a regular person and not a crazy man with an ax. "Seems almost alive, doesn't it?"

"It is alive."

"It can't be alive. It's made of metal and wood."

"Where do you think wood comes from?"

"Trees?" She backed closer to the door. Soon she would be close enough to break and run. She might make it to safety before he caught her.

"Exactly. Trees are as alive as we are."

Two more steps. She whirled, bolting towards the door. He didn't bother following her. No footsteps sounded in her wake. As she swung the door open, she glanced over her shoulder.

Archie wasn't after her. He was climbing up on the platform, ax at the ready. His target was the golden horse. Penny felt the creature's panic as if an invisible cord bound them. Terror, and a memory, flickered at the corners of her mind.

"No!" Time seemed to slow as Penny retraced her steps. Her progress felt slow, as if she were running uphill, even as the invisible connection between her and the horse propelled her forward. "You can't. We protect her, care for her."

Archie turned, his face a snarl of rage. "To what end? So she can suck out every ounce of energy we have, every drop of blood. So she can control every aspect of our lives until we end up like my dad, old and worn and having lost everything important he ever had in his life?"

"He spent his life caring for the carousel. It was his life's work, and he did it gladly." As she would, if given the chance.

"He chose this monstrosity over me, his own son." Archie's voice rose, and his eyes were wild and bloodshot.

She was on familiar ground now. Her own father had always put his next scheme over the welfare of her and her sister. "He talked about you, before you came. He wanted to see you. Maybe he even regretted past decisions. But I think he did his best and what more can we ask of people?" Her dad had told her the same.

Archie lowered the ax, tapping it against his thigh. "You think you're special because he offered this to you. His life's work. His legacy."

"Only because he couldn't find you."

"You're too blind to see he was handing you a curse, not a gift. A curse which has haunted my family for years and still won't let go. Even though she had a new slave to do her bidding, she wouldn't let me leave. I don't know how she did it, but I know she's the reason I ended up at the foot of the stairs. I could have broken my neck. The shock killed my dad."

Penny hadn't heard about Archie's fall. "I'm sorry you got hurt, but I don't see what the carousel has to do with it. Your father was an old man with a heart condition. I've done nothing to you, but you could have killed me and my friends by tampering with my car. And when that didn't work you tried again, shooting me on the trail."

He snorted. "If I wanted you dead, you'd be dead. I was trying to save your stupid hide, but you wouldn't listen."

"Funny way of showing it." He obviously didn't care if she died, but if he didn't actively want to kill her, maybe she could talk him down. She'd called the park before leaving Little Hills. Surely someone would be here soon. If they listened to the message. And believed what must have sounded like a hysterical, disgruntled former employee.

"Get out while you can. I'm going to do what I should have done years ago. The curse ends tonight." Archie turned his back on her, and marched towards the golden horse, the beating heart of the carousel.

Penny raced forward, leaping the steps to the platform in a single bound. As Archie raised the ax, about to lower it onto the neck of the horse, she jumped on his back, raining blows with her fists.

Knocked off balance, he missed the horse and fell forward, the ax banging against the platform. Penny landed on top of him, cushioning her fall and knocking the wind out of Archie.

He flailed for a moment as she rolled off him and grabbed the ax. He caught a handful of her shirt and yanked. She landed heavily on her knee, pain exploding in the joint and radiating up her wounded arm. But she kept her hand on the ax.

She crawled forward, cradling the ax next to her body. Archie's hand closed over her leg, and she kicked as hard as she could. He screamed, and she pulled free, crawling another foot towards the golden horse. She grabbed the wooden stirrup and struggled to pull herself to her feet. Her knee still blazed with pain and her arm burned, but she stood, her weight supported by the horse. She could feel the burnished wood pressed against her chest as she leaned against it, but she smelled horses, a sweet scent of sweat and hay. And beneath it the faint whiff of trees and fresh air. She reached for the horse's mane with her sore arm, feeling the coarse hair beneath her fingers even as the wood refused to yield. She met the horse's eye, painted, but seeing, and a wave of strength flooded her body despite her injuries.

"I won't let you hurt her."

Archie had also regained his feet, and although he was panting, he towered over her and probably outweighed her by almost one hundred pounds. "You can't stop me."

Penny had the ax. But for how long? Unless she could land an initial disabling blow, Archie would take it from her. And she didn't think she could hack someone, even if she held on to it.

"Let it go. Go back to your old job. Falling down the stairs was just an accident. The carousel doesn't have any supernatural powers."

Yeah, right, the smell of horses was stronger, and a breeze caressed her face. "The carousel is a historical treasure. Damage it and you'll go to jail."

"I must break the evil."

Penny ran. She couldn't defeat him in combat, but without the ax there was little he could do to the carousel. She jumped off the platform and ran flat out towards the door. Archie's feet pounded behind her. He was gaining on her.

She burst through the door and into the parking lot. If she could make it to Marjory's car, she could get away.

She hadn't taken two steps when Archie tackled her, grinding her into the pavement and jolting the ax from her grip.

Archie went for it, stepping on her in his haste to get it. When he turned, ax in hand, she thought she was dead, but he ignored her battered body and went back into the building.

She had to get back on her feet, had to stop him. She drew herself to her knees, but could no longer put any weight on her injured arm. Pushing with her good hand, she tried to stand. She got one leg beneath her before swaying like a sapling in a heavy wind.

"Penny!"

Someone was calling her name. Had the park department finally arrived? Strong arms encircled her, pulling her the rest of the way to her feet.

"Are you okay? What happened?"

Gage. Tears of relief slipped from her eyes. She wasn't alone anymore. "Archie," she managed. "He's got an ax. He wants to—" she couldn't even put it into words. "Stop him."

"Call 911. But don't worry. I've got this."

***

Gage awoke with a roaring headache and the image of a bloody ax fixed so firmly in his mind it felt as if someone had actually buried the blade in his skull. The image was clear and the pain visceral. He sat up, clutching his head. His questing hands found nothing, no ax, no gaping wound.

He moaned, trying to remember where he was, what he was doing. It came to him in broken fragments. Wanting to feel whole again, to help Penny. The feeling he was running out of time. And deciding to try the experimental treatment. Steve and the lab.

He couldn't think with the pounding in his temples, but he recalled driving to the agency, talking to Steve, and drinking the watermelon-flavored elixir. He was in the recovery room. Had it worked? Steve had said something about running tests, but he didn't feel capable of using even his basic five senses, much less extra ones with his crushing headache. Headaches were one of the most common side effects he'd read about in the literature.

"Hey, you're awake." Steve appeared in the doorway and flipped on the lights.

Big mistake. Gage closed his eyes against the daggers of pain triggered by the brightness. "Turn it off."

Steve hit the switch again, plunging the room into shadows. It wasn't fully dark. Light from the lab spilled into the space. "Headache? Here, drink this." He pressed a glass into Gage's hand.

It had a medicinal smell, like cherry cough syrup. Nausea swirled in his stomach. He didn't want to drink it, didn't want to subject himself to another round of visions. But if it would dampen the pain in his head... Gage took a sip, and then drained the glass.

Within a few minutes, it took the edge off. He could make out shapes in the dimness, another couch on the other side of the room, and the silhouette of his buddy in the doorway. "The tests?"

"They recommend doing them immediately if you're up to it. Then after twenty-four hours and finally at one-week intervals until the effect diminishes."

"*If* it diminishes." Gage wouldn't have taken the drug if it didn't hold the promise of a permanent cure.

"That's the goal, of course, but we've not yet achieved it on any of the test subjects."

But Gage wasn't trying to gain a new ability, he was trying to restore one he'd been born with. He had to hope it gave him an edge. "They weren't psychic."

"Most were not," Steve agreed. "But some were low-level psychics."

The pain reliever hit Gage's system like alcohol on an empty stomach. The ache took another step back. "I think I can manage a few tests."

"Great. Let me set up a basic screening."

Gage followed Steve into the lab, blinking at the harsh glare of the lights. Steve sat at a computer and tapped on the keyboard.

The image of an ax formed again in Gage's mind. The ax looked old, scuffed from wear, and spotted with rust. But fresh blood glistened on the edge, shining bright red as it trickled down the paint-chipped handle.

"Did you send me an image after I took the potion?"

Steve looked up from the computer screen. "No. Almost everyone experiences vivid dreams, but we don't direct them. They appear unique to the individual, although one of my colleagues is tracking them to see if they form a pattern. What did you dream about?"

"Floating up into the clouds, lots of noises and smells. Drifting towards the sun." He left out the intense heat and fear of incineration.

Steve nodded, his attention back on the screen. "I haven't read all her research, but you're not the first to have an out-of-body experience."

A drop of blood fell from the ax and splattered on the floor of the lab. But when Gage pointed it out to Steve, it disappeared.

"A bloody ax."

That caught Steve's attention again. "I think that's a first, but one guy fought a space battle with lasers."

Splat. Another drop of blood, there, then gone.

Gage's stomach tied in a knot. He wasn't a wannabe Jedi warrior dreaming about the Force. He'd faced real challenges, both in the field and since his injury, with Penny and Ben. If Steve had not sent the image of the ax, something else had. A flicker of his old ability, seeing something that existed elsewhere? Or a hint of precognition brought about by the drug? Whose blood was on that blade?

Splat.

This time the blood didn't disappear, but Gage knew Steve could not see it. It was a message for him alone. "Penny."

"I'll set you up in one of the remote viewing chambers and have one of our operatives send you some data."

"Penny's in trouble."

"What?"

"The ax. You didn't send the image. I pulled it on my own. The drug worked, but I've got to go." Go where? Had he seen something else in the vision? A blurry image of a carousel?

"Wait, if you think it worked, it's important we test right away. We need all the information we can get to tweak the formula."

"No time. Send backup to Faust Park." Gage ran from the lab. Steve called something after him, but Gage didn't listen. He poked three times at the elevator button, cursing its slowness. What if he was already too late?

Ding. Gage scurried into the elevator and pushed the button for street level. It seemed to take forever to climb a few floors. When he exited, he forced himself to walk at normal speed. He shouldn't even be without an escort since he was here as a test subject and no longer had the authority of an agent. If he drew too much attention to himself, and the agency held him, he wouldn't be able to help Penny. He prayed Steve wouldn't call security. If he did, Gage would never get to Penny on time.

Once in the parking lot, he ran to his car and tore off, tires squealing. Penny shouldn't be at the carousel. She'd lost her job and should be at home, resting her arm. The doctors told her not to drive. But still, he worried she had gone out to the park and was now in danger. He glanced at the clock on his dash. He'd been unconscious longer than he realized. No one should be there, much less Penny and an ax-wielding Archie. The carousel was closed.

But the fear didn't lesson, and he pressed his foot harder on the accelerator. Penny was in danger. He'd fought against his attraction to her, had tried to be happy for her and Ben when they were dating. He'd told himself that he was too old for her, that he was her boss, that she deserved someone whole, not an agency reject.

He'd never even kissed her.

He intended to remedy that lack if they got out of this alive. Whatever "this" was. He thought about Juniper's research into the haunted dolls. Was the carousel, or specifically the one horse, inhabited by a ghost or demon? The agency was need-to-know only, so he didn't have too many details, but he had heard they dabbled in more than psychics and magic.

He took the turn into the park too fast, nearly spinning off the road. Dusk was falling, signaling the end of park hours. He passed one car in the outer lot as he hurtled towards the inner. The tightness in his chest eased as he saw only an old truck and an unfamiliar car parked by the building. No sign of Penny's car.

But then he saw the figures struggling on the ground. He slammed to a stop and jumped from the car as the larger figure, a man, kneed the woman in the back, reaching for something. Then the man lurched to his feet, holding the ax from Gage's vision, identical but for the absence of blood.

Gage froze. He would never reach Penny in time. He couldn't move fast enough. But to his astonishment and relief, the man lifted the ax and turned toward the building.

Gage ran to Penny and swept her into his arms. "Are you okay? What happened?"

"He's got an ax. Stop him."

"Call 911. I've got this." Gage hated to leave her. Blood stained the bandage around her arm, and scrapes covered her face and hands. But she appeared relatively unharmed. Archie had returned to the building with the ax. Was someone else at risk?

He ran after the other man. Inside, he scanned the area quickly, but saw no one except Archie, now on the platform, ax raised over his head.

"No!"

Startled, Archie swung his head towards Gage. But his arms continued their downward arc, the blade smashing into the horse with a sound of cracking wood.

An echo of sound, like the shrill whinny of a horse, assaulted Gage's ears. A fountain of blood sprayed from the wounded animal, coating the platform. Gage feared he would slip in it as he came after Archie, but it was there and then gone. Illusory blood, like the splatters in the lab.

Archie struggled to pull the ax free, but it stuck in the shattered horse. In the second before Gage reached him, he abandoned the weapon and fled.

Gage followed, close on his heels. They ran out of the building towards Penny. Gage couldn't let Archie get there first. He was just a step behind as they burst through the door, but Archie bolted straight for his truck, ignoring Penny.

Gage let him go. Penny still stood where he had left her, but had crumpled in on herself, holding her stomach as if she had internal injuries. Remembering how Archie had ground his knee into the small of her back, Gage feared she might. He held her close as Archie's truck roared past.

"Did he kill her?" Penny asked, face white.

Gage barely noticed the use of the feminine pronoun. It seemed fitting, somehow. "He got one blow in. That's all. She will be fine." Now he was using the pronoun. He remembered the blood and assured himself it was fake, an illusion brought on by the drug he had taken.

Penny shuddered. "We have to help her." She pulled free of his arms.

"Stop. We need to get you to a doctor. Then we will call the park department and report the damage. This isn't your responsibility anymore, remember?"

Penny's face hardened as she nodded. But as he helped her to his car, she directed one last longing look at the building housing the carousel. Gage slammed the door shut and turned at the sound of an approaching vehicle.

Steve rolled down the window. "Looks like I missed all the fun."

Chapter 17

Once again, they treated and released Penny at the hospital. A doctor restitched her arm, while a nurse applied fresh bandages, and treated the worst of her scrapes and bruises.

"We've got to stop meeting like this," said a nurse, who had also been on duty during Penny's first visit. "You are giving this place a reputation for violent crime. Usually our emergency cases are accidents and illnesses."

"Just trying to shake things up."

The nurse, a middle-aged woman with a sweet face, eyed her sternly. "This was the same man who shot you?"

"I didn't actually see who shot me, but yes, I think so."

"You need to get a restraining order."

"A piece of paper doesn't provide much protection, but I hope the police will catch him." Belatedly, Penny realized the woman suspected Archie was a stalker or rejected suitor. She wondered what the nurse thought about Penny coming in with a different man this time. "The man is not my boyfriend. He's a colleague." It was the best explanation she could come up with. If she started talking about haunted carousels or family legacies, the woman might call the psych ward.

"You need to get another job."

Penny didn't argue, but she worried about what would happen to the carousel now. They would have to close the ride until they could repair it, but who would become the new operator? Worse, what if they decided the repairs were too expensive or that two crimes on park property made it unsafe for children? Would the carousel find another savior, as it had after The Highlands closed, or would it molder away in storage?

"We've called in two prescriptions for you this time. More pain medication and an antibiotic. The doctor doesn't want to risk infection from your fall in the parking lot. You're good to go," the nurse said.

Gage waited for her in the waiting room. Steve had arranged for her to give her statement to the police tomorrow.

"I borrowed Marjory's car. We need to get it back to her."

"Already taken care of," Gage said. "I'm going to take you home and this time you're going to follow doctor's orders."

Penny didn't argue. Every part of her body hurt. "Have the police notified the park department?"

"Yes, after securing the scene."

"How bad is the damage?"

"Archie only got one blow in, but it cracked the wood. I was a little busy trying to stay alive, so I didn't pay that much attention."

"Do you think they will fix it?"

"Sure. The carousel and the Butterfly House are the park's chief attractions, although the village is also popular."

Penny closed her eyes. She had to let it go. The park department had fired her. It was no longer her responsibility or concern. Right. "Will the police catch him?"

"Archie? Probably, if he stays in town. But he lives a fairly transient life. They might not pursue him if he takes off. All they have on

him now is property damage. They want to question him about the shooting, but don't have any actual evidence against him for that or tampering with your car."

Penny wanted to know how Gage had known she was in trouble, but could barely keep her eyes open due to shock and the pain medication the hospital had given her.

"I'm going to swing by the pharmacy to get your prescriptions before dropping you at home. I'll call you tomorrow."

Penny nodded. It felt good to let someone else take charge. She must have fallen asleep, because the next thing she knew, Gage was pulling up in front of her house. He walked her to the door and under his watchful gaze, Dora didn't even scold, although she pursed her mouth in disapproval.

Penny thought she might let go when they were alone in Penny's room, but her sister limited herself to one parting shot. "You're going to get yourself killed if you can't break whatever hold that carousel has over you. I should know. An angry ghost possessed me, too."

Penny didn't answer, although she wanted to protest that the situation was different. Nobody possessed her. But she couldn't deny the link between herself and the golden horse. And Juniper thought an evil entity might possess the horse. She turned her face to the wall and pretended to be asleep.

Dora sighed and turned out the light.

Within minutes, Penny was no longer pretending.

***

When Penny awoke the next morning, the sun was already high in the sky. She had slept peacefully, with no dreams that she remembered. It

hurt to move, but her cuts and bruises weren't as painful as the night before. Her arm, however, throbbed worse than when she was first shot. She dutifully took her medications and made her way downstairs.

Gage sat on her couch, reading the thriller she'd seen sitting by his bed. Had he been there all night?

"How are you feeling?" He slid a piece of paper into the book to mark his place.

"Okay, I guess." As good as possible, considering her physical injuries and the anxiety which gnawed at her insides.

"We're going to go to the police station and then I'm taking you to lunch."

He drove to St. Louis county, where Penny gave the police an abridged version of what had happened. She touched lightly on her foreboding, saying she'd wanted to visit the carousel, where she had worked for a couple weeks, as a rider, just to make sure the new operator knew what he was doing. She didn't mention getting fired and hoped the police officer wasn't aware of the real reason behind her supposed resignation.

"I hit some unexpected traffic and by the time I got there, they were already closed. However, the door was open, so I went inside. I wanted to make sure he hadn't forgotten to lock up."

"And that's when Archie Jenkins chased you with an ax?"

"Yes, I saw he was about to damage the carousel, and he didn't want any witnesses. He would have killed me if Gage hadn't shown up when he did." Penny wasn't sure that was true. Archie had seemed more concerned with ridding himself of the golden horse and its influence than harming Penny. But it made for a good story and might draw some attention away from the weaker points of her tale.

"And you believe he is also the man who shot you?"

Penny nodded.

The police officer shook her head. "It makes little sense, but the information we've dug up on him shows he has issues with people in authority. No arrest record, however."

"My sister saved his father's life and the old man befriended us. I think Archie is jealous of that friendship." More half truths.

"Motive, perhaps, but his behavior is still very erratic. We put a warrant out for his arrest, but he seems to have gone to ground for now." The police officer needed no more information from Penny, so she thanked her for coming in and let her go.

The suburban police station was clean and nondescript, unlike the gritty urban station where the police had taken Penny after her arrest. Still, she was glad to step out into the bright sunshine. The windows of the building felt like eyes boring into her back as she and Gage walked to his car.

"If you've no objection, I thought we could get another picnic and go to Faust Park," Gage said.

"The carousel?"

"Is closed. I checked the website."

Penny frowned. She should have thought of that. "Does it say why?"

"Closed for refurbishing. Doesn't say when they expect to be open."

"Then why do you want to go there? Are you trying to draw Archie out?"

"No, he wouldn't dare show himself anywhere near the park. I think he's far away by now."

If he can leave. But now that he's shown himself to be a threat, won't the horse want him gone?

"I thought we could visit the Butterfly House. You seemed to enjoy the one at the zoo."

They picked up Chinese takeout and carried it over to the picnic tables. Penny expected to feel drawn to the carousel building, but although she was aware of it, it left her alone, allowing her to enjoy the weather and the time with Gage.

"You saved my life. How did you know?" she asked, ready to face what she'd been too tired to deal with last night.

"I'm not sure your life was in danger, but I saved the carousel from worse damage."

"He would have killed me after he destroyed the carousel. But you're avoiding the question. Marjory said you were out sick."

"A white lie. Since Steve cleaned up after us, you probably already guessed I was at the agency. I wanted to try an experimental drug. It worked. I got a clear vision of Archie's ax."

"That's great."

"If it sticks," Gage agreed. "So far the longest it's lasted in any of their test subjects is about a month."

"Can you keep taking it?" She tore open a packet of soy sauce and added it to her rice.

"Three trials are the maximum they are allowing right now. It's a new drug, so there aren't any long-term studies. And there are side effects."

"Like what?"

"Varies per person, but I got a killer headache. If Steve hadn't given me something to counter it, I wouldn't have been able to help you."

"I'm grateful you arrived when you did." Without Gage's intervention, she felt sure Archie would have hacked the horse to pieces and maybe her as well.

"So, bottom line, I'm excited about the drug, but worried its effect is only temporary."

They finished their food and drinks and walked over to the Butterfly House to buy tickets. The large glass structure stood on the edge of a pond. The building cast a reflection onto the water, a rippled, blurred duplicate of itself.

Inside, it was humid, but probably a few degrees cooler than outside. Once again, Penny found herself charmed by the delicate winged beauties. She stayed still until one landed on her hair.

"It probably thinks you're a flower," Gage said.

"Take a picture," Penny urged. She almost wished Ben was there to immortalize her and the butterfly, but having a third person along would spoil the romantic mood.

Gage snapped a photo and the butterfly flew off. They moved on. Penny took a few pictures of her own. "I should find out what some of these plants are and plant them in my garden. I'd love to attract more butterflies." Penny had never planted a garden before moving into the house she shared with Dora. As a child, they had moved too often to bother. When they had moved in with their grandmother, Penny had occasionally helped with her grandmother's prized roses and her herb garden, but now that she had her own place, she'd planted flowers out front and tomatoes in the small backyard. As a beginner, she chose flowers that were easy to grow. But she would experiment more next year.

"There is a gift shop. I'm sure they have books in there, maybe even some starter plants."

"Good idea." It was the middle of the afternoon on a workday, and only a few people wandered around the greenhouse. A bored-looking attendant had most of her attention on a group of kids who were darting around while their mothers kept half an eye on them and chatted amongst themselves. No one was watching Gage and Penny.

Gage placed a hand on the small of her back and steered her towards the part of the conservatory which overlooked the pond. A few tall trees provided privacy.

He reached up and touched her hair. "I thought I'd lost you. I broke every speeding law to get there, but worried I wouldn't make it in time. When I saw you lying on the ground, that monster on top of you... I didn't know if you were alive or dead." His finger traced her cheekbone.

"I'm fine. I just tore my stitches and got some cuts and bruises."

"What were you really doing there? I didn't think you would ever want to see the place again after how the park department treated you."

"I had a feeling the carousel was in trouble."

"You saw it in the cards?"

"I didn't even need the cards. I just knew something was wrong. Since you rarely call in sick, I went to your house to check on you. You weren't home, which worried me, but then my vague uneasiness became crystal clear. The carousel needed me right away."

"It's unnatural to feel such attachment to an inanimate object."

"It feels alive to me."

"We should have Ben try again to contact the spirit."

"He may never want to come back here after breaking his wrist." Penny struggled with a sense of guilt. "I should have called him, asked how he's doing."

"You've been busy."

True, but she should have found the time.

"Thanks for checking up on me. I shouldn't have lied about being sick and just said I was taking the day off. Guess I'm still not quite used to being the boss." His blue eyes darkened and Penny swayed towards him.

He reached for a lock of her hair. "You have the prettiest hair I've ever seen."

Penny's breath hitched. "Dora's is thicker and a deeper color."

"Yours is like butterfly wings. Soft and fragile." He closed the slight gap between them, and his lips found hers.

His mouth was soft, warm, and knowing as it pressed firmly on hers. She fell into his embrace, her breasts pushing against the hard wall of his chest. He was a man in his prime and, from the feel of his body, must spend some time working out. Heat tingled in her veins, and she splayed her hand against his chest, feeling the muscles flex beneath her fingers. For a moment, she forgot where they were. She wanted to devour him, to peel the tee shirt from his body and trace every inch of him.

Fortunately for her, Gage broke the connection and stepped back. His gaze smoldered, and Penny saw her own passion reflected within. But he had a clearer head. At any moment someone might turn the corner and stumble upon them.

Penny blinked and tried to collect herself.

"I've been wanting to do that for a long time," Gage said. The corner of his mouth twitched up as if he realized how deeply his kiss had affected her.

She drew her hands into fists so she wouldn't reach for him again. What was wrong with her? It was just a kiss, though a skilled one.

He took her hand, smoothed out the fingers. "Have you seen enough? Should we check out the gift shop?"

No, she hadn't seen nearly enough. But there would be time for that later. "Sure."

They wandered hand in hand back through the conservatory and over to the gift shop. As Penny browsed through the books and plants on display, she kept one eye on Gage. When he thought she wasn't looking, he rubbed his forehead near his temples. She guessed he still had a headache from the experimental drug. Was it safe? No one really knew.

She picked a plant and took it up to the counter. She didn't recognize the older woman who checked her out and didn't think they had run into each other during her brief stint as the carousel operator. The Botanical Garden, not the park department, ran the Butterfly House. She wondered what these employees knew about the vandalism at the carousel last night. They probably knew it was closed.

When Gage turned towards the car, Penny motioned for him to follow her. She led him to the carousel building, skirting the patch of parking lot where she had fallen last night. A sign on the door said the carousel was closed for maintenance until further notice. She pressed her face up to the tinted glass, but couldn't make out the carousel. Gage stood a few steps behind her. She felt his gaze on her back.

She could probably put her hand to the card reader and open the lock. She wanted to see just how much damage Archie had inflicted on the horse. But no one had questioned her story about the door being open and she wasn't sure she was ready to share the truth, even with Gage just yet.

"We'll figure it out."

She stepped back with a sigh. "I'll ask Ben to try again. I don't think you should take any more of that drug. Who knows what it might do to you."

Gage stiffened. "It's my best shot. I was foolish to think I could discover a cure on my own. I don't have a scientific background."

"Let them work out the kinks first. I don't want them using you as a guinea pig."

"We should get going. I need to check in at the restaurant."

Reluctantly, Penny headed towards the car. "I'm serious. I'm not sure I trust the agency."

"Maybe you just don't want any competition." Usually, he opened the door for Penny, but this time he walked straight to the driver's side, got in, and slammed the door. Penny fumbled for the passenger door with her sore arm and climbed in.

"Are you serious? I read tarot cards. I've never attempted remote viewing or had any interest in it."

Gage pulled into the street. "I not only saw the ax, but knew you were in trouble. That's getting into precognition, your territory."

"If the drug gives you extra abilities, that's great. But precognition isn't always an easy burden to bear."

Gage drove in silence for a while. "I don't get it. I will do whatever it takes to regain my paranormal abilities while you don't even use yours to the fullest advantage."

Penny stared at the hard line of Gage's jaw. He seemed nothing like the man who had held her tenderly last night or kissed her in the conservatory's corner. "You know why I quit reading the cards. But I've taken them up again. I'm doing my best." But was she? She thought about her reluctance to explore whatever strange affinity she had with electricity.

Gage wouldn't hold back if he suddenly had extra powers. But he had his secrets, too. He had told no one, even her, about trying the experimental drug. Why was she even considering a relationship with a man who didn't seem to trust her?

"Just take me home." She didn't need to be clairvoyant to know she wouldn't be kissing him again any time soon.

Chapter 18

D ora wasn't at home when Gage dropped Penny off. She wanted someone to talk to, but was relieved not to have to admit to another troubled relationship. Her family didn't do well with matters of the heart. Her grandmother had never married, although she never lacked for male companionship. Even now that she was in her seventies, she dated frequently, sometimes seeing men younger than herself.

Penny's parents had married, and when she was young, she'd thought them a happy family. But she'd been a child with a child's perspective. There must have been problems she didn't see, which were bad enough for her mother to abandon not only her husband, but her children as well.

Dora had fallen deeply in love while still in high school, but first love had not been strong enough to withstand the damage wrought by disability and broken dreams. Penny had always liked Win and thought he might have stuck by Dora, even with her hearing loss, if the accident had not shattered his own dreams of a professional baseball career along with his bones. As it was, the double loss had been too much for him, and he had eventually stopped calling. Like Dora, he had a long road to recovery, but had left for college before her sister.

Penny's boyfriend resented the time she spent nursing her sister back to health and helping her cope with her disability. He'd whined so much that by the time he dumped her, Penny had been more relieved than hurt, but he'd taught her how selfish some men could be. Not all. She knew there were good men out there, but the experience soured her on love. Penny wasn't sure she could escape the cycle.

Plato was excited to see her, and Penny allowed the dog's affection to soften the sting of Gage's accusation. She understood his frustration. She'd been proud, arrogant really, when she first discovered her talent with the tarot, but after failing to foresee Dora's accident, she had wanted to escape the responsibility. Gazing into the future wasn't an exact science because the future was not predetermined. Every action a person took altered his destiny. She stressed this to all her clients. She could only tell them the probable outcome if they continued on their same course. Seeing something that might come to pass differed from seeing something real in the present moment.

Doctor's orders were to rest, but Plato hadn't had a walk in days unless Dora had taken him. He behaved well on a leash, rarely pulling, so Penny decided she could manage a walk without further damage to her arm.

Plato wagged his tail as she hooked him up. She had just locked the door and started down the walk when Dora pulled up in front of the house.

"Where have you been?" Penny asked. "Studying with a friend?"

"No." Dora exited the car and fell into step with them. "I was helping Ben out with a client shoot. He's having difficulties working with his arm in a cast."

"I should help him. It's my fault he got hurt."

"That's not the way he tells it. He says you warned him not to climb that tree."

"But it's my fault a mad man shot at us."

"Hardly. Archie is responsible for his own actions." Dora reached over and took the leash from Penny. "I can walk the dog. Go home and get some rest."

"I need to clear my head." The girls walked in silence for a while. Days were long this time of year and they still had hours of light, but the temperatures had dropped enough to be pleasant. Once they reached the tourist area, others joined them, some out for a stroll, and some going to the bars and restaurants. Plato strained at the leash when he saw another dog, and Penny was glad her sister had taken over.

"Of course, if you listened to me in the first place and turned down the carousel job, none of this would have happened," Dora said, giving Plato a sharp yank.

"Here we go."

"I wish we'd never gone out to the park. Wish I'd never saved Mr. Jenkins' life. What good did it do? He died soon after, anyway. I know what you told me about getting to see his son again, but look how that turned out? The man's a raging psycho who wants you dead."

At least she isn't blaming me for causing Mr. Jenkins' heart attack by getting a splinter. "I should have stayed away. Usually I want nothing to do with the paranormal, except for reading tarot cards. But from the beginning I felt connected to the carousel and whatever entity inhabits it." *Linked by blood.*

"So you think something possesses the carousel, like the dolls Juniper told us about?"

Penny shrugged. But it was the closest she could come to an explanation.

"Then maybe it's a good thing Archie destroyed it."

"I'm sure the park department will repair it."

"But should they? It's dangerous."

"It's not dangerous." *Except maybe to the caretaker.* "It's a beautiful piece of history. Have you ever considered that some of its charm comes from the underlying consciousness inside?"

Dora gave her a look. "Do you know how crazy you sound?"

"Says the girl who was possessed by a two-hundred-year-old spirit."

"All right. If you say something is there, I believe you. But you need to leave it alone. I'm sure Gage will let you have your job back."

Penny snorted. She hadn't forgiven Gage and wanted to tell Dora what he had said. However, her sister didn't know about the agency or Gage's former paranormal abilities. Penny had sworn to keep the agency secret and wouldn't betray Gage's confidence, even if she was mad at him. "I've still got my job, but Gage thinks I'm as crack-brained as you do. He's angry I visited the carousel yesterday, although I didn't know it would put me in danger." *More lies.*

Dora drew to a stop and put her hands on her hips. They stood outside a bar and grill, and the enticing aroma of hamburgers wafted from the open door. "Don't tell me you've broken up with Gage, too?"

Penny lifted her brows. "I thought you didn't approve. You went on and on about him being too old for me and how he was my boss to boot."

"Ben was clearly the better choice, but I want you to be with someone. I don't want you giving up your life to take care of me. I needed your help at first, but I'm doing fine now."

Penny frowned. "You're doing great. I never meant to imply otherwise. Do you wish I hadn't moved here with you?" Not that Dora could have talked her out of it.

Dora rolled her eyes. "No, stupid. I enjoy living with you. It's not as good as living in the dorm, but it's much better than staying with Grandmother and going to the local college."

"Then what's the problem?"

"You push everyone else away like you want it to be just the two of us. Forever."

Penny stepped away from the restaurant door to allow a couple to enter. She started walking back towards home, unsure if Dora would even follow. "That's not fair. I encourage you to make friends."

"I'm not talking about me." Dora turned back, too, although Plato looked disappointed. "You don't have any real friends from work except Gage, and now you might have ruined that. Ben was perfect for you, but you kept him at arm's length."

"I get along just fine with people at work. I just don't want to spend my free time with them. And until Ben figures out his feelings for Juniper, he shouldn't be in a relationship with anyone else."

"Maybe, but I think you used Juniper as an excuse."

"I don't see you dating anyone."

"I'm not ready. But at least I admit it."

Penny hated what Dora left unsaid. That she might never be ready. Penny didn't want to believe it. She believed in second chances. "Maybe I'm not ready either." They hadn't had the best role models.

Dora slid her free hand into Penny's. "Try harder."

Penny muttered an agreement.

***

Penny called Ben the next morning and offered to help him out in the studio.

"Won't that be like the blind leading the blind?"

"Between us we have two good arms. I feel bad you got hurt."

"You got shot. I was just my usual clumsy self, falling out of a tree. But if you're up to it, come on over."

"Can you come get me? Dora took the car to school."

Ben agreed. When they got back to his studio, they worked together to set up cushions, boxes, and a baby friendly backdrop.

"Dora told me what happened to the carousel. Why were you there? Archie could have killed you."

"I knew it was in danger. There's something there, although it may not be a ghost, which could be why you sensed nothing unusual."

"You want me to try again. Why? Usually I have to convince you to investigate."

"I'm drawn to the carousel, perhaps in the same way Charlene and Victoria called to you."

Ben adjusted one of his lights and stepped back to survey the results. Satisfied, he moved on to the next. "I was way over my head with Charlene. Finding the proof I'd been looking for fired me up, but I didn't know what I was doing. Who knew a ghost could possess a living person? My actions could have cost Dora her life."

"It was unfamiliar territory for all of us. I didn't want to believe in the existence of ghosts, but the dreams terrified me. I had never experienced anything like them before."

A box slipped from Ben's bad hand and landed on the floor at a drunken angle. Penny straightened it.

"You weren't curious to learn more? I can see how it might have been scary, but wasn't it fascinating to get a glimpse into their lives?"

Penny heard the hint of longing in Ben's voice. He would appreciate the dreams, and she'd be happy to hand them over to him if she could. Why were all the men in her life drawn to the parts of her that made her uncomfortable? Well, if she was honest with herself, she'd never want to lose the precognitive ability which gave her such an advantage in her tarot readings. But the future was changeable. The past had already occurred. She felt helpless, knowing she could do nothing to avoid the coming tragedy.

And they were so realistic. She experienced the victim's pain and terror along with them. Sometimes she feared she would not wake up and would remain forever in another person's life. "It's not like watching a movie," she tried to explain. "I feel as if I am the other person."

"Charlene had a lot of rage."

Not so much in the dreams. Hurt, yes. Anger at the way people treated her. But the rage had come after her lover's father betrayed her. Two hundred years of being shut up in Sycamore House had exacerbated that rage. "She had her reasons. But dealing with the spirit world can be dangerous."

"I sensed nothing malevolent about Victoria. After what we went through with Charlene, I understood your reluctance to get involved, but I had to help her."

"Exactly how I feel about the carousel."

Ben nodded, although he still appeared confused. "You've had dreams about a specific horse?"

"I've had dreams about horses and the golden carousel horse in particular. I've taken to thinking of her as Goldilocks."

"Goldilocks is the same horse Archie tried to chop into firewood? He must know something about what is going on."

"He must. Along with his father before him. Maybe even his grandfather who carved the horse."

"Could the grandfather's spirit possess the horse?"

"I don't think so. I've had no dreams about him."

Ben glanced at his watch. "We can go over to the carousel this afternoon, but my first client will be here soon."

"Should I stay and help?" She knew Dora did so, changing the sets between takes.

"No. One gimp is bad enough. Two might scare off my customers. I'll come by after lunch and pick you up. Do you need a ride back to your house?"

Penny didn't want to risk him being late for his appointment. "No, I'll walk."

When she stepped outside, she was glad of her choice. It was early enough that the heat was not oppressive, although it promised to be a hot day. She even stopped by the bakery and treated herself to a cinnamon roll.

When she got home, she drew a tarot card. The Nine of Cups. She frowned. The card was a good one, symbolizing abundance. The man in the card had enough wealth, power, and wellbeing to get off the treadmill of life and take a well-earned rest. He looked happy, if a bit smug, about it. Unfortunately, it didn't seem to apply to her life right now, although if it showed her future, she'd take it. However, she knew happiness had to be earned. It wouldn't just show up without effort on her part.

Could it mean she and Ben would successfully contact whatever lived inside the golden horse? Her fingers felt icy as she tucked the cards back into their bag. The air conditioner was on, but they kept it set to an environmentally responsible level and the room wasn't cold.

After lunch, Ben picked her up. Back when they were dating, he would probably have suggested going out to eat, but it was better that they didn't. As angry as she was with Gage, she didn't want to complicate things.

When they arrived at the carousel building, Ben slapped the heel of his hand against his head. "I should have realized they'd be closed. I'm not sure I'll be able to pick anything up out here."

Penny chewed her bottom lip. "You think you'd have a better chance if we were inside?"

"Of course, but I don't think anyone is going to let us in even if they have a key."

"I can get us in."

"Really? Did they forget to disable your key card?"

"Something like that." Penny considered sending Ben back to the car on a made up excuse, but changed her mind. She closed her eyes and again tried to picture the wires running through the key reader. She placed her hand over the box and heard the clunk as the lock released. When she opened her eyes, Ben was looking at her in amazement.

"Handy trick."

"I've only used it on this door. I'm not a master thief."

"Calm down. I'm not accusing you of anything."

"We'd better go in before someone notices us and wonders what we're doing here." They slipped in, and Penny strode straight to the golden horse, wincing at the damage done to it. The ax had bitten into the horse's shoulder, creating a nasty gash. Penny's own wounded arm twinged in sympathy.

"She's in distress. They didn't even cover it up."

Ben stepped up beside her. "Possessed or not, it's still made of wood. I don't think it can feel."

Penny hoped he was right. "What do we do next?"

Ben pulled a short, stubby candle out of his pocket. "We hold hands and I try to make contact." He lit the candle with a lighter and placed at the foot of the golden horse. Then he and Penny sat on the edge of the platform and took hands.

"Spirit of the carousel, I reach out to you. We'd like to talk to you."

"Tell her we're sorry she got hurt," Penny whispered.

Ben cleared his throat. "We're sorry that man hurt you, but the park department will fix you. You will be good as new."

Penny glanced over her shoulder at the candle. She thought the flame jumped, but couldn't be sure. She looked over at Ben. His eyes were closed, his features taut. She wanted to ask him what he felt, but didn't want to interrupt him. As for herself, she felt only the ache in her arm.

Ben sighed. "I'm not getting anything."

"That's okay. It was worth a try." Penny wasn't sure if she was disappointed or relieved. She leaned over to blow out the candle.

"Wait."

She froze.

"Hello? Who is there?" Ben looked up at the ceiling. "I'm listening. Are you trying to speak to me?"

A thread of sound came so softly that Penny almost thought she imagined it.

"Disappointed."

"Why are you disappointed?" Ben asked.

"My son. Penny. Mostly my son."

Penny's breath caught in her throat. "Mr. Jenkins? I'm so sorry about what happened to you. And about what I allowed to happen to the carousel."

"Penny risked her life to protect the carousel," Ben said. "Your son tried to destroy it. Why?"

A sigh, like the rustling of dry leaves in the fall. "He wants to escape his duty. I tried to pass it on to Penny. She likes Penny, finds her worthy. But finding someone else to oversee the carousel didn't release my boy from his duty. She doesn't let go easily."

"What do you mean?" Penny knew Mr. Jenkins referred to Goldilocks.

"Walk away if you can. I should not have recruited you. It's a terrible burden. I fear for Archie. She will take revenge."

"How? The carousel is an inanimate object. Isn't it?"

No reply.

"Mr. Jenkins, your son has been hurting people. First, he damaged the brakes in Penny's car, then he shot her, and finally he threatened her with an ax when she tried to keep him from vandalizing the carousel. The police don't know where to find him. Do you know where he might be?"

Penny waited thirty seconds. "Is he gone?"

"No, but I can barely see him. He may not have the strength to speak."

Or he doesn't want to. While she appreciated his concern for his son, she thought the carousel was in more danger from Archie than the other way around.

Finally, the ghost spoke again. "We used to live near The Highlands."

"Do you think Archie might hide in his old neighborhood?" Ben asked.

"Maybe he was right. Maybe he should destroy it."

Penny bristled at the change in pronoun. Goldilocks was distinctly female.

"You spent your life caring for the carousel. Why would you want your son to ruin it?" Ben asked.

"It was a waste of a life. I didn't see that until it was too late. She grows too powerful."

"What should we do, Mr. Jenkins? How can we help you and Archie?" Nothing. Ben waited a few moments. "He's gone."

"Are you sure?"

"Before I could see the faint outline of a man by the controls. It's no longer visible, but I suppose he could still be here, listening."

Penny shivered. She'd liked Mr. Jenkins in life and didn't exactly fear him in death, but she would never understand the straightforward way Ben accepted his ghostly friends.

"He's only been dead a short amount of time. It takes a while to build up the power Charlene possessed." Ben seemed to read her thoughts.

"Thanks for doing this. It didn't occur to me we might encounter Mr. Jenkins."

"Sorry I couldn't reach Goldilocks. She either doesn't want to make herself known or she is not a ghost."

Penny didn't think a person inhabited the horse. She thought it something else entirely. She turned towards the candle, but it was already out.

"Did you blow the candle out?"

Ben shook his head.

"I didn't either."

"It was probably a draft, although I guess Mr. Jenkins might have been able to do it."

Goldilocks had done it. Without fanfare. Penny lifted the candle and sniffed it. It smelled of lavender. And ancient forests.

Chapter 19

After leaving Penny at her house, Gage drove to the cafe, gave the place a cursory overlook, and retreated to his office, slamming the door behind him. What had he been thinking, to accuse Penny of being jealous of his powers? She'd been nothing but sympathetic about his loss and her resentment of her own powers appeared genuine, although he suspected she might feel differently were she actually to lose them.

He'd been projecting his own feelings onto her. He *was* jealous of her ability. It made his own loss more painful. But now she was angry with him and justifiably so. He'd just gotten so angry when she told him not to take any more of the experimental drug. She didn't seem to realize how important it was to him to be whole again. Had he not taken the drug, she might be dead, and Archie would have ruined the carousel she cared so deeply about.

He paged through his own research, searching for an enhancing spell. Until their association with Ron, Gage had been purely science-based. He had put little stock in magic, despite the research being done at the agency. Ron had convinced him that magic was real. It might have some scientific explanation. Gage had always believed so-called paranormal abilities were rooted in science, just science they couldn't yet explain. He now collected spellbooks. His search yielded nothing about an enhancing spell, but one of his books mentioned that quartz was an amplifier.

He stopped by a metaphysical store on his way to the agency and chose a lovely crystal with a hint of green and slid it into his pocket.

Steve led him to his office. "Ready to do some testing?"

"I want to take another dose."

"No way. No one has ever taken it a few days apart and we haven't even had time to test your last dose. We know it worked initially, but I want to see how long it lasts."

"Taking it more often could be the way to maintain potency."

"Or the way to fry your brain."

"I need to do this."

Steve shook his head. "I can't allow it. Maybe if you were still part of the agency."

"They kicked me out." Realizing he was bouncing his knee up and down, he forced himself to still.

Steve leaned back in his chair and laced his fingers behind his head. "That's what you've told me, but they offered you a desk job."

"I only lasted a few months as a pencil pusher. I need to be in the field."

"Let the redhead manage your restaurant, do some paperwork, and take part in the official trials. It's your best chance to get your mojo back."

"Her name is Penny."

"Just trying to get a rise out of you. Are the two of you dating yet?"

Gage thought about the kiss they had shared, the sun warm on his back, the perfume of flowers in the air. "She's in danger, and I can't help her if I can't see what's going on."

"I understand the police are still looking for the guy who shot her and tried to chop up the carousel. What does he have against your girl?"

"He thinks she stole his job."

"Running the carousel? There has to be more to it." Steve dropped his hands in his lap and leaned forward.

Gage nodded. "The carousel seems to be haunted by some sort of malevolent presence."

"A demon?"

Gage shrugged. As far as he knew, the agency had never found any proof that demons existed. But he'd left over a year ago, and the agency was a notoriously secretive place. "Are they real? Have you dealt with one before?"

"Never seen one, but there is plenty of anecdotal evidence."

Gage studied his friend's face. If Steve *had* dealt with a demon, the agency would have sworn him to secrecy. Once, Gage had trusted Steve with his life. While in the field, they had each other's backs. But though Gage felt sure Steve wanted to help him, he might not be willing to share agency secrets. "Any anecdotal stories which seem pertinent?"

"I'll let you know if I hear something. Now, are you willing to do some testing?"

"Sure." Going back down to the lab would offer him his best shot at nabbing another dose of the potion.

***

That night as they ate dinner, Penny told Dora about helping Ben stage his photo shoot, but didn't mention them going out to the carousel and contacting Mr. Jenkins' spirit. The older man's death still upset Dora. She had saved his life only to have him lose it a few weeks later. It made her question the value of her skills.

Penny assured her sister she had done her best, but Mr. Jenkins' passing made her think about fate. She might tell her tarot clients they created their own futures—and fully believe what she taught—but sometimes she couldn't dismiss the influence of destiny. It seemed some things were meant to happen.

After dinner, they took Plato for a walk and then watched some TV. Penny was about to get ready for bed when Dora announced she was going out.

"Some friends and I are doing an escape room."

Penny told her sister to have fun and went on up to bed. It was good that Dora was going out. She shouldn't be hanging out with her sister all the time. But being alone made her miss Gage all the more and worry that their relationship was over almost before it began. Why had he kissed her one moment and the next accused her of being jealous of his ability? She didn't want to keep him from regaining his remote viewing skills. She only wanted to keep him safe.

She swallowed a pain pill to help her sleep, changed into the tee shirt she wore to bed and climbed beneath the sheet. Although the air conditioner was on, it was too hot for blankets. She turned off her alarm, since she had no commitments for the next day. As her arm's lingering soreness faded, she drifted off.

Another fire burned in the grove of the woods, but this one was small, barely melting a ring in the frost covering the ground. No one danced. No music or chanting filled the air. Instead, a few people, faces drawn with hunger and cold, circled the meager flame. They spoke, keeping their voices low. It was a secret meeting, unknown to the rest of the tribe. Times were hard. The winter had been long and showed no signs of ending. Food was scarce and sickness stalked their group.

They entreated the trees, especially the eldest. Why had she withdrawn her protection? What could they do to win it back?

They all knew what the answer would be. Even before they'd traveled to the grove under cover of night, they'd known. The question was less what needed to be done than who would make the sacrifice. For in the most desperate of times, the trees called not just for blood, but for life itself.

The first to be considered were some of the tribe's less able and valuable members. But this posed a risk that the sacrifice would not be enough. The gods demanded the best.

Some thought it should be a young maiden. Beauty exchanged for prosperity. Others suggested an elite athlete whose loss they would feel during summer hunts and while fighting with other tribes.

The chief let them talk, although he knew he would never make it back down the mountain. It was his responsibility to take care of the group. He would be the one to make the sacrifice worthy of a god.

"Enough," he said at last. "I offer myself to the goddess. It will appease her."

He saw the hope and relief on the face of the other elders. The goddess would shower them with blessings for the sacrifice of such a high-status individual. They had not known if he had the courage to put himself forward. He had not known with certainty himself, though he'd known it was his duty.

The spiritual leader nodded, face calm and expressionless. "We thank you. I will prepare."

The chief knew the old man would go off alone and fast, although they all went hungry now. The shaman would make a potion for the chief to drink to ease his terror and suffering as the goddess took her due.

There would be flames. And blood. And in the end, hopefully, peace.

Penny lurched to a sitting position, her breath coming fast. They were coming for her. They would kill her, burn her, snuff out her life so the others could live.

It took a few moments for her to realize she was once again back in her own body, safe in her room. Chilled despite the warmth of the room, she pulled up the blanket she'd tossed aside earlier. Nausea churned in her stomach and she could only be grateful she had awakened before they killed the body she inhabited.

Human sacrifice. She knew many cultures practiced it or had before modern laws forbid it. She flipped on the light, unsure if she could fall asleep again. Unsure if she wanted to.

A restlessness filled her body. An insistent tug in her chest. She wanted to go to the carousel. Wanted to care for it. To heal it.

To kill for it?

Penny shoved the thought aside, appalled it had even entered her conscious mind. She had no desire to harm others. After years of caring for her sister, she'd recently expanded her circle to include Ben, Gage, and even Juniper. She ran her tarot business with complete transparency, fighting every day not to sink to her father's level. She went to great trouble never to misrepresent what she could do.

The tug came again, like a lasso around her heart. The ax had torn through the wood of the golden horse, maiming it. It needed blood to heal, to survive. To thrive.

Penny glanced at her watch. It was after midnight. She could drive over to the park, cut her arm, and sprinkle blood over the gaping hole. She couldn't actually fix the horse. The park department needed to hire a woodworker to repair the damage, but she could do her part.

She climbed from bed and dressed in a tee shirt and shorts. She was tying her shoes when the realization hit her. It would not be enough.

The horse, or the entity inside the horse, wanted more than a sprinkle of blood. She wanted a river. She wanted a life.

Penny's fingers froze on her shoelaces. No. She wouldn't sacrifice her own life or take another. Maybe Archie had been right. Perhaps the golden horse was evil. Should she have let Archie hack it to pieces?

She should go back to bed, pull the covers up over her head, and ignore the horse's commands. An image flickered in her mind. The carousel going faster and faster, spinning so fast it flung riders from their mounts. The glass door shattered. Shards of glass as sharp as knives flew, one lodging in a young woman's chest. The woman staggered, hands wrapping around the glass as she tried to pull it free. She slumped to the ground, blood pouring from her wound and pooling on the floor. Blood everywhere.

"Stop it. Someone will repair you. I promise. If the park department doesn't have the money, I will raise it somehow. You don't need blood. You need wood, glue, paint, and a skilled craftsman. Murder and mayhem will do nothing but seal your doom." She didn't know if the horse could hear her, but she spoke aloud, even as her thoughts swirled with the possibility of finishing what Archie had started. She couldn't believe that the man who had nearly killed her twice might have had the right idea, but the violent visions chilled her blood to slush. It moved sluggishly through her veins.

Everything would have been fine if Archie had never returned. If Archie had not damaged the horse, she would not be calling for the ultimate sacrifice. She would have been content to take the odd bit of blood now and then, as she had for years.

Children crying. People screaming. The roar of distant flames. She was hungry. Oh, so hungry.

The noise faded along with the blood-soaked vision. The rope around her heart eased, the knot pulling free. Her breath returned to normal. Warmth stole back into her limbs. The compulsion to race to the carousel vanished. Penny sat on the edge of her bed, fully dressed. It was still dark outside, and the park was closed. Besides, they had fired her. The carousel was no longer her responsibility.

Moving slowly, like a sleepwalker, Penny removed her shoes and lay back, fully clothed, on the bed. She would get a little more sleep, prepare to face the day. The carousel had caused her enough problems. No more. She could resist its call.

***

Steve put Gage through a battery of tests. It became immediately apparent that his ability to see things at a distance had returned, although not as strong as before. This wasn't the first time. He had seen the bomb on the Sunflower Showboat, but could not duplicate that result in the lab. Now the lab results were encouraging, but whether the effect would last was another question.

He scored statistically above average in a card guessing game, where he predicted what suit would come up, but the results weren't astounding. Gage was inclined to dismiss it, but Steve assured him it was significant, if underwhelming.

He displayed no ability to pick up on the thoughts of others unless they were in the same room with him. Even then, it was slight.

"You might pick up on body language, but I don't think you are telepathic," Steve said.

Gage thought mind reading would be a handy skill to possess, but he couldn't imagine the thoughts of other people constantly bombarding him. The uptick in clairvoyance intrigued him, but it was the remote viewing he sought. The ability to see and know things at a distance had been a part of him since early childhood, and he felt blind without it.

"This is all very encouraging," Steve said. "I don't know why you resisted coming in for so long."

Because he didn't want to be a lab rat? As badly as he wanted to regain his abilities, he didn't fully trust the agency. "There haven't been many human tests."

"All the more reason we need you." Steve smiled. "Although I guess I can understand why you wouldn't want to be first."

If not for Penny, he would have waited longer. Keeping her safe was his top priority, but he couldn't deny the glimmer of success excited him. If the potion restored his power, the agency would take him back. "So let's step it up. Give me another dose."

Steve's smile faded. "I'm not allowed to do that."

"Live on the edge. Isn't that what you've been telling me to do?"

"I've asked you to join the trial. Not take senseless risks."

"Just give me some off the record."

Steve set his jaw. "Enough, Gage. I can't. That you're asking me to do so, shows you've lost perspective."

What Gage felt he was losing was time. When another agent stuck his head in the room, distracting Steve, Gage swiped a vial from the refrigerator. He did it so smoothly he decided he'd missed his calling as a pickpocket. He allowed Steve to walk him out of the building, grumbling slightly to not raise suspicion.

Once in his car, he took a peek at the tube. He hadn't had time to be picky, and this one glowed blue instead of red. A different formula or just a different flavor?

He'd find out soon enough.

Chapter 20

A rchie was getting too old to be sleeping on a park bench. He'd slept on plenty in the early days after running away from home, but while then it had been an adventure, now it was just uncomfortable. He was hiding out at the park where the carousel had given rides to hundreds of children between its time at The Highlands and its cushy new digs at Faust Park. During the day, he spent time in malls, restaurants and libraries. Anyplace with air conditioning where he could blend into the crowd. When those places closed, he came to the park. Fortunately, it cooled down at night, but it was still muggy, and the bench felt hard as a rock. He'd lost count of the number of mosquito bites he had. Sometimes he slept in his truck. The seats were more comfortable than hard benches, but it was stuffy. He preferred sleeping under the stars.

If it hadn't been for Penny and her boyfriends, he wouldn't be in this mess. He'd abandoned his hotel room and everything in it after the shooting. He knew she'd given his name to the police. The shooting had been a mistake, anyway. Messing with her car had been good. No one could trace that back to him. It was a clever, if not foolproof, way to get rid of someone. He hadn't wanted to kill her, just put her in the hospital for a while or cause her so much inconvenience she gave up on the carousel job and left his father alone.

He just wanted to go home, but the entity had shown him she meant business by coming after him and his father. Trying to leave had cost his dad his life, and Archie had nearly broken his neck. So he had cut the brakes on her car and shot at her in the woods. He should have dug for dirt first. Almost everybody had something to hide if you looked hard enough. The juvenile arrest had worked like a charm.

He slapped at a mosquito and shifted position as one of the wooden planks dug into his shoulder. If she hadn't interfered, he would have destroyed the cursed horse and finally rid himself of the evil which had stalked him his entire life. Even now, hot, sweaty, and itchy, he remembered the rush of power he'd felt when the ax shredded the wood. Penny must have called for backup. A man had come after him. Not the same man she'd been hiking with. She appeared to work her wiles on any man she came in contact with, including his own father. Though his dad had been glad to see his long-lost son, Archie resented the affection his old man had shown that stupid girl.

He had to regain access to the carousel. And this time maybe he wouldn't use an ax. He would use his favorite tool. Fire.

He drifted near sleep, imagining piling brush against the wooden horse, dousing it with gasoline and setting it alight. The fire would glow red and orange, eventually engulfing the entire carousel and spreading to the building. It would crack and roar like a living thing, devouring all in its path.

Once he burnt the horse to ashes, it could no longer hurt him. Or could it? No, he had to believe the power the entity possessed would disappear once its base disappeared.

He turned over, but it was useless. There were no comfortable positions on the bench. Maybe he should have killed Penny when he had the chance. One blow from the ax was all it would have taken. He'd gone too easy on her, drawing the line at murder. She deserved to die for cozying up to his father, stealing his family legacy, and protecting the carousel at his expense.

He sat up, giving up on sleeping. His fingers tingled as a sense of urgency overcame him. His feelings pulled him in opposite directions, part of him wanting to claim his family legacy while another part tried to run as far from it as possible. He'd hated how his father had put the welfare of the carousel above that of his own family and how he'd been content, happy even, to work a menial job all his life as long as he could serve the golden horse.

Archie didn't want to serve anyone or anything. He'd been afraid of the entity's power, but that might have been a mistake. He should embrace the power. Feed it. Control it.

He felt the horse reaching out to him, demanding he repair the damage he'd caused. She was weak and needed help. Needed to draw upon the life force of someone else. He could help. Deliver Penny into her clutches. But not out of love for the old ride. No, his help would come at a price. He would feed the beast only if the beast fed him in return.

He should tell the park service that Penny, angry at being fired, had tried to destroy the carousel. Not him. She was lying about what happened. He would have to get rid of her boyfriend, too, but with a second sacrifice, the entity's power, and Archie's, would skyrocket.

He would have a true partnership with the carousel. He would hunt down every boss who'd ever belittled him, every girl who'd ever turned him down and sacrifice them to the entity. As it grew in power, the carousel would draw visitors from all over the world. He would rise in the ranks of the park department, gaining influence and money. His efforts would turn Faust Park into a major tourist attraction, rivaling the zoo and the Arch. He'd never sleep on a park bench again.

Life would be good. Better than it ever had before. Archie had loved his dad as a boy. Even looked up to him when he was very young, but the old man must have been a fool. How could he have stood on the sidelines, watching and protecting the carousel when he could have been harnessing the power for his own ends? His grandfather must have seen the potential. Why else would he have chopped the tree down and carved it into a work of art?

Archie returned to his truck. He'd swapped license plates with another vehicle to keep the police off his tail. It wouldn't work forever, but it bought him some time. He needed to prepare for the sacrifice. Fortunately, he knew where she lived.

***

Gage drove straight home from the agency. He didn't know how long it would be before someone realized he'd stolen the vial, but he had a rough plan in mind. He would take the potion and go into a darkened room as he had while at the agency. When he awoke, he would try to locate Archie, if the knowledge hadn't already come to him.

He wasn't sure what he should do next if he discovered where Archie was hiding. He'd like to inform the police, but he wasn't sure they would take him seriously or react quickly enough. Vandalism wasn't a high priority case, but it might help that Archie was also a suspect in a shooting.

In the end, he decided he would phone in an anonymous tip to the police, but would also go after the man himself. He couldn't count on the authorities to take care of the threat Archie presented.

The decision made him nervous. Although he'd done field work for the agency, he'd always been behind the scenes, watching everything from afar. It had seemed safe, but he had found out the hard way that others could harm from a distance as easily as he could view.

He owned a gun and had a license to carry, although he rarely used it for anything but target practice. He took it from his safe, loaded it, and placed it inside his shoulder holster on the bathroom counter. A weapon might even the playing field.

He was as prepared as possible and could no longer put off the inevitable. He uncapped the blue vial and drank the contents. This time it tasted of blueberries, with a similar bitter aftertaste. He hoped it was the same formulation as before, or one that worked even better.

He barely made it to his walk-in closet before collapsing on the pile of blankets and pillows he'd set up earlier. He lifted his foot, which felt weighted down with an anchor, and kicked the door closed. Darkness descended, and he fell into a nightmare.

This time he didn't float. He burrowed. Like a drill, he spun round and round, twisting into the earth. Pressure built in his lungs. He could barely breathe, and when he did, it tasted of mud and decay. His hands tore at his throat as he gasped for air. Sweat pooled on his forehead as it grew hot. He must be near the core, the molten metal center of the earth.

Was it the province of hell? Gage considered himself a spiritual but not a religious man. He'd never really believed in a physical hell ruled over by a devil with pitchfork and horns. But as his skin burned, he wondered.

Just when he thought he would fall into a pit of lava, the earth let go and he slipped into a cooling lake. He flailed about, thrashing to the surface where he took in deep lungfuls of air. He lay floating in the body of water for a long time, taking shuddering breaths.

But just as the burning in his lungs faded, sharp talons grabbed him by the ankle and yanked. He tried to kick free, but with a yelp he went under. Water closed over his head, blessedly cool, but as impossible to breathe as dirt. The pressure built in his lungs again, more quickly this time. The creature clawed at his ankle, and pain shot up his leg. He reached down to pry it loose, but his strength ebbed as the blood trickled down his foot. Whatever had hold of him was going to drown him in this subterranean lake. His lungs were bursting, a white light filling his head.

Part of him knew he was still in his closet, but he wasn't sure it mattered. Encroaching death felt all too real.

***

Archie would take care of the boyfriend first. He could handle Penny, but although he outweighed the younger man, he wasn't in as good of shape. If he had the element of surprise, however, he thought he could take him.

After an hour of research on his computer, Archie found a photo of the man alongside an article written about a new restaurant he was opening. Once he had a name, it took only a few minutes to find an address. The man didn't live far from Penny. After crossing the river, they would both be within his grasp.

Archie parked his truck a few doors down from the address he had found online. The front windows were dark, and he hoped Gage was asleep. He debated about bringing his rifle, but the gun wasn't good in close quarters, and the sound of a shot would draw unwanted attention. If the man was asleep, he could slit his throat.

No!

Archie felt the negation like a punch to the gut. The entity didn't want him to kill Gage here and waste his blood. She wanted Archie to bring the sacrifice to her and spill his blood at her little wooden hooves. But Archie would do whatever he wanted to do.

No.

"I'm bringing you the girl," he said. "This is just clean up."

The greater the sacrifice, the greater the power.

Archie tried the front door. Locked. He was about to go break a window when he noticed the pots on either side of the door. He kicked one, wincing at the clatter it made as it fell over. Nothing. He kicked the other, exposing a key.

He let himself in. For a few moments, he stood in silence, allowing his eyes to adjust to the darkness. For a big man, he could move with stealth. He'd first learned how to blend in while living on the street. Even when his situation improved, he'd found it handy to know every inch of the theme parks where he worked, along with the quickest route from one place to another and the little hidden places where he could eavesdrop on conversations between coworkers. He'd heard a few juicy nuggets over the years, which had given him leverage when it came time for annual reviews or when he wanted to trade hours with someone.

Flipping on a small flashlight, he tiptoed through the first floor. Living room, dining room, kitchen, and bath, all empty. He took the stairs to the second floor, pausing as one creaked underfoot. At the top of the stairs he paused, listening. Two doors stood open. Archie checked them first. A full bath and a small room outfitted with a desk, computer, and bookcases.

He opened one of the closed doors and saw a double bed, a chest of drawers, and a chair by the window. A landscape painting hung over the bed, but otherwise the room was impersonal. A spare bedroom.

That left the master bedroom. If Gage was home, he was in there, probably asleep. Archie put his ear to the door. He didn't hear snoring or any other sound. He wrapped his fingers around the flashlight, blocking most of the light, and opened the door.

A king-sized bed dominated the room, which also held two nightstands, a chest, and dresser, a TV mounted on the wall, and yet another bookshelf. Seemed the dude liked to read.

From his position at the door, the bed looked empty. Archie crept forward. The covers were smooth and untouched. The adrenalin rushing through his veins popped and fizzed. Gage wasn't home. He was a loose end Archie would have to come back and fix later.

Maybe he was with Penny. That would make things more difficult, but not impossible, especially if they were asleep. Archie pictured the couple sprawled in bed together, the bright red of Penny's hair cascading down her bare shoulders. Could he manage with a knife? He might need a gun. A quick shot to the head would take down Gage. Penny would scarcely have time to wake up before he had a knife to her throat.

No.

The damn voice again, insistent like the itch of the mosquito bites he couldn't stop scratching. But he would not listen. He was going to do things his way.

No longer worried about covering the flashlight, Archie checked the attached bath. Empty, as he expected. But something sat on the counter. He trained the flashlight on it. A gun, tucked neatly in a holster. Archie couldn't believe his luck. He took the gun and slipped it into his pants pocket.

There was one more door, likely leading to a closet, and he almost left it alone. At the last minute, he gave into curiosity. He wanted to know what it was about a guy like Gage that could attract a woman like Penny. Archie supposed he was good looking enough. It might be a cliche, but women went for tall, dark, and handsome. But the guy in the woods had been just as good looking, and younger. He thought women were more into men who enjoyed sports, rather than books, but then again, what did he know. His track record with girls wasn't that great.

He opened the door and shined his light on parallel rows of shirts and pants. There was no apparent organization. Casual pullovers hung next to dress shirts and jeans paired with slacks. Shelves stretched above the clothes rods. A handful of boxes lined one, while the other held a jumble of carelessly folded sweaters.

This was a pointless exercise. Looking at the man's clothes wasn't giving him any insight into how Gage attracted women, although Archie admitted his own wardrobe could use an update. He didn't see any beer-stained sweatshirts hanging in Gage's closet.

As he stepped back, the beam from his flashlight illuminated the floor. What he had taken to be a pile of pillows and blankets held something more. Gage slept there, his breath shallow. Under the glare of the flashlight, his skin looked gray.

What the hell? The man had a perfectly good bed. Why was he sleeping in the closet like a vampire? He grabbed for the gun, dropping his flashlight. Gage didn't stir. Keeping the gun trained on the sleeping man, Archie retrieved his flashlight. He took a step closer. Was the man already dead? Had someone done his dirty work for him?

No, Gage was still breathing, but Archie had seen his share of drug overdoses during his years working in theme parks. Both customers and employees sometimes overindulged. Usually someone found them in the bathrooms, a gruesome scene for the finder. Archie had cleaned far too many bathrooms in his time, but preferred operating the rides to cleaning, retail, or food service.

He hadn't figured Gage for a drug user, but you couldn't always tell. The man looked like he was going to die. All Archie had to do was leave him here and no one could contradict his story about what happened the night he chopped up the carousel. True, both Gage and Penny had already given their statements to the police, but once they were both dead, their words wouldn't carry as much weight. Especially since Gage's death would expose him as a junkie.

Or he could bring him along. Gage couldn't put up a fight in this condition. Could the entity still absorb Gage's power if he died of an overdose rather than violence?

Bring him.

Archie tucked his flashlight away, flipped on the lights, and hoisted Gage over his shoulder. Ugh. The man was heavier than he appeared. One down. One to go.

Chapter 21

T ry as she might, Penny couldn't go back to sleep. The compulsion to go to the aid of the golden horse, to even kill for her, had
lessened, but not entirely evaporated. It seemed almost as if the horse
knew she'd pushed too far and had backed off.

But tension still strummed along her nerves. Something was wrong.
She got up and peered into her sister's room. The faint light from
the streetlights was enough to see Dora sleeping with her dark red
hair spread out on the pillow, one hand resting by her head. Without
her hearing aid, she wouldn't wake unless Penny turned on a light or
somehow activated the sixth sense everyone possessed to some extent.
The sense that allowed you to "feel" the weight of unseen eyes.

She wandered into the hobby room and pulled a tarot card. It was
the High Priestess. Penny often associated this card with herself, since
she possessed intuitive abilities beyond the average. As she stared at
the image of the woman on her throne, a scroll in her lap, she couldn't
help but feel she needed to act. But how? What exactly did the tarot
want her to do?

Her sister was safe. Who else might be in danger? Gage? Ben? It was
the middle of the night. Both should be sleeping. Both had been in the
car with her when the brakes failed and Archie had shot at Ben, but

both times Penny was sure she had been the primary target. Archie had no reason to go after anyone other than Penny.

Or did he? Gage had kept him from destroying the carousel. She rubbed the High Priestess card between her fingers. Archie knew how to hold a grudge.

Reluctantly, Penny opened the lower drawer of her desk. Her crystal ball rested there, wrapped in a silk scarf. It was a gift from her great-grandmother, whom she could barely remember. The woman had died when she was very young. Her great-grandmother had also possessed clairvoyant abilities, and she had predicted baby Penelope would follow in her footsteps. She had left Penny the crystal ball while passing down her secret recipe for her healing balm to Pandora, who hadn't even been born. She'd left it in trust for future descendants since her lawyer told her she couldn't name someone in her will who didn't yet exist. The lawyers may have thought the old woman was crazy, but on her sixteenth birthday, Dora had received a sealed envelope from their great-grandmother's estate. She'd signed a non-disclosure agreement before the lawyer handed it over.

Even when she'd been high on her success with the tarot cards, Penny had avoided using the crystal ball. At first she had spent hours staring into its milky surface, but she rarely saw anything but a swirl of colors, perhaps brought on more by eye strain than psychic ability. Even when she saw something, she rarely knew what it meant. But the ball had shown her Dora's face when Charlene's spirit had possessed her. Penny feared what she might see in the ball, but her fear of losing someone she cared about won out.

She lifted the ball from the drawer, along with its stand. She carefully set the ball on the stand and lit a brace of candles around it. Then she sat down and stared.

She tried to focus on the crystal in front of her, but her mind ran wild. Was this how it was for Gage when he did remote viewing? Images had come for him once, but now he experienced this same frustration. Perhaps she'd been too quick to dismiss the new drug. She'd been trying to protect him, but some risks were worthwhile.

Something swirled in the glass. She saw a burst of fiery color, followed by serene and cooling blues. A figure formed within the swirls. A beast sprouting horns and grasping something in its talon-like hands. Was that Gage, limp as a rag doll in the beast's claws? Penny grasped the ball and leaned in closer. Yes, she recognized Gage, despite the gray cast to his features.

The tinkling sound of shattered glass broke her concentration. Her hands dropped from the ball. The noise had come from downstairs. Seconds later, she heard a bark, followed by a yelp. Plato.

She reached for her phone to dial for help, but she wore only her nightshirt and had plugged her phone in on her nightstand.

She blew out the candles, waited a moment to give her eyes time to adjust and slunk down the hall. She'd go to her room first and call 911 before checking on Dora and Plato. Perhaps she should hide in her closet, but she couldn't get the sound of Plato's yelp out of her mind.

Back to the wall, she crept down the hall. The door to her room was open, just as she'd left it, the black interior yawning like the mouth of a cave. She slipped inside and knocked her knees against her bed. Trailing her fingers over the mattress, she moved towards her nightstand. She had nearly reached it when something hit her from behind.

A cry of pain escaped her lips, and she stumbled, falling half onto the bed. Her flailing hand reached for the nightstand. Her fingers hit the edge, but couldn't grasp it. Blackness stole her consciousness.

***

Archie raised the gun, ready to hit her again, but Penny lay still. He flipped on his flashlight and smirked at the sight of her sprawled across her bed, hand reaching for safety. Not that she would have found it. He'd already taken her phone and thrown it across the room. One by one, he was taking out her defenses. He'd broken the back door. The dog had been a surprise, but he'd kicked it, sending it flying several feet before following up with a blow to the head.

Then he'd searched the place as he had Gage's house. He'd left the sister alone, for now, and while it had initially dismayed him not to find Penny in her room, he'd caught the whiff of candles. Alerted to her presence, he'd heard her stealthy movement down the hall and ambushed her just as she thought she was safe.

He'd come prepared and bound her arms and legs with duct tape, as he'd done to Gage. Slinging her over his shoulder, he carried her downstairs, panting under the weight, although she was a small woman. Kidnapping people was hard work. He'd dragged Gage most of the way and had barely hoisted him into the truck.

He stopped at the bottom of the steps for a moment to regain his breath and shifted Penny's weight to a more comfortable position. He'd parked a few doors down, away from the streetlights. Upon reaching the truck, he flung Penny's body into the bed next to Gage. Then he pulled a tarp up over both of them.

He got into the driver's seat, pulled away from the curb, and headed for the carousel. As he drove, he considered how he should make the sacrifices. A bullet to the head would be easiest, but he didn't know if it would satisfy the entity's craving for blood. He could use his knife, but thoughts of fire enticed him. Fire was cleanest of all, and if he set his captives alight at the foot of the horse, he might just take her out with them, stealing all the power for himself. For all his blustering, he wasn't sure he could control the ancient evil.

He drove carefully, not wanting to get pulled over with victims in the back of his truck. However, there was little traffic in the middle of the night and he soon arrived at the park. He left the truck in his usual spot and encountered his first obstacle. The building was locked, and his key card was disabled. The door was metal, the windows thickly paned with glass that wouldn't break easily. If he still had the ax, he might have been able to chop his way through, but hitting it with the butt of Gage's gun would not work. Should he try the tire iron from his truck or shoot the card reader? He figured a bullet would disable the reader, but wasn't sure if that would open the door. A broken card reader might just make it impossible for anyone to get in.

Penny's key might still work, but he hadn't brought her purse and didn't think she carried it in her pajamas. Did he actually need to be inside the building? Could he make the sacrifice from here?

No.

She wanted the victims inside, where she could soak up their blood. Closer now, he felt more of her hunger, a gnawing in his own gut. And a hint, just a hint, of anger. She wouldn't be so ravenous if he hadn't hurt her. He shivered, momentarily glad of the thick metal door between them. But then she had somehow thrown him down a flight of stairs from miles away. He didn't think a door could protect him.

He raised the gun and fired it into the glass. The bullet pierced through, and cracks radiated from the hole. Then he went back to the truck for the tire iron. When he shifted the tarp to reach his toolbox, he met Penny's fierce gaze. She was awake.

"What are you doing? Why have you brought us here? You know the police are looking for you."

"Shut up."

She kept her gaze level with his, but despite her bravado, she looked pale. Archie would bet she had a good idea why he had kidnapped her.

"We have to help Gage. Look at him. Something is wrong with him." She struggled against her bonds. "Just cut me loose and I'll take care of him."

"In a few minutes it won't matter. All he has to do is hang on until I get him inside."

"Listen to what you're saying. You were right. The horse needs to be destroyed. I was wrong to stop you. She is evil. Let me go and I will help you get rid of her. You and your family will never have to answer to her again."

He opened his toolbox and rummaged around until he found the tire iron. "We were both wrong. It's better to harness the power than destroy it."

"Archie, you're not a murderer. You wounded me that day with your rifle instead of going for a killing shot. Once you cross the line, there's no going back."

He hesitated. He cared little for most rules, but he'd never taken a life. For several nights after starting the fire at The Highlands, he'd experienced nightmares. They'd only ceased when he learned no one had died in the blaze. But he'd been young, then. Soft. Life had hardened him. The entity had driven him to this point.

He pointed at Gage. "I didn't do nothing to him. He did this to himself. All I need to do is dump him at her feet."

"You're still contributing to his death. And what about me? I just befriended your dad when he was sick and lonely."

"Befriended him, my ass. You tried to steal him away from me." He leaned in, putting his face close to hers. She wrenched her head back, slamming it into the bed of the truck. "You were happy enough to take my family legacy from me, but now you're going to feed it. My father didn't know what he was dealing with. I'll do more. I'll do better. And it will be all thanks to you and lover boy here."

A tear trickled down Penny's face. "Resist her. She came after me, too, but I held out. Don't allow her to control you."

He slapped her, thudding her head against the truck bed again. "You know nothing about me. I'm in charge here. I don't take orders from women or amusement park rides."

"Then prove it."

Grabbing the tire iron, Archie stalked back to the building. He bashed in the fractured glass, gathering strength with every blow. Once he cleared a large enough area, he climbed through, nicking his shoulder on a shard he'd missed. He cursed at the sharp pain, muttering under his breath as he hurried towards the yellow horse.

She watched him, painted eyes alert and glowing faintly red.

"I'm here and I've brought the man and the woman." He laughed, catching the hungry gleam in her eye. "Yeah, you may not like it, but you'll take what you can get." He glanced at the gash in her side, which almost appeared to ooze blood. He hurried back out to the truck.

He brought Gage first, straining under the man's weight. He barely made it up to the platform and was wheezing by the time he dumped Gage's lifeless body by the horse.

Untie him.

"Are you crazy? What if he regains consciousness?"

He looks dead.

Archie placed his fingers on Gage's neck. It took a while, but he eventually found a thready pulse. "He's still alive."

Then release him. A bound victim brings less power.

"Fine." Archie took his knife and sawed through the duct tape. He thought Gage too far gone to resist, but sighed as the last of the tape fell away and Gage didn't move. He exposed Gage's throat and prepared to make the cut, a trace of nausea uncurling in his belly. "Do I say a spell or anything?"

Wait. Get the girl first.

Relieved by the delay, Archie left Gage where he lay and went back for Penny. This time she struggled as he threw her over his shoulder, making it more difficult to carry her. But she was lighter than Gage, and although his heart labored, he wasn't breathing hard by the time he dumped her on the platform.

"You want them to bleed out, right?" He pulled his knife out and reached for Gage. Penny screamed and thrashed on the platform.

Untie the girl.

"No. She's awake."

Although he hadn't turned on the carousel, suddenly the lights flared, music poured from the speakers, and the platform revolved. Thrown off balance, Archie pitched to the side, dropping his knife. The knife hit the platform with a clatter and spun off onto the floor.

"Stop. I did as you asked. Why are you making this difficult?" Did the thing want blood or not? He scrambled to his feet, jumped off the platform, and retrieved his knife. The platform spun faster, and the horse remained eerily silent.

Somehow, despite her bonds, Penny had wormed her way to a sitting position. Placing her feet against the floor and her back to the yellow horse, she was attempting to stand. Archie hurled himself at the spinning carousel, grabbing at the fleeing animals. He missed and crashed back to the floor.

He regathered his strength and pushed forward with a roar. This time he grabbed the tail of a horse and held tight, dragging himself aboard. He lurched across the platform towards Penny and the yellow horse. Somehow, despite the centrifugal force, she had reached her feet. Archie closed in on her even as Gage rolled off the platform and onto the floor, head cracking on the floorboards.

Penny threw her hands up in defense as he approached. She'd used the horse's jagged wound to saw through the duct tape, although from the amount of blood dripping from her wrists, it had come at a cost. Her feet were still bound, however, and she couldn't escape him.

The lights flickered, and one burst, raining glass down on the platform. The music faded away, and the platform decelerated, still spinning, but with each round slower than the one before.

Archie grabbed one of Penny's arms and although she pummeled him with her free hand, he held her at arm's length, and her blows barely grazed him. He would start with her.

Give her a choice.

"First or second?"

Him or her.

"I thought they were both on the menu."

A blast of air, warm and fecund, hit him like a brick wall.

Him or her.

***

Penny's wrists burned like fire and from the pain in her arm, she knew she had torn her stitches loose once again. Gage hadn't moved, not even when he fell off the platform, and she worried he was dead. If Archie were to be believed, he had not harmed him. Gage must have taken another dose of the drug.

Her panic spiked when she saw Archie put his knife to Gage's throat. Although she wasn't touching the outlet, she mentally reached for the circuits of the carousel, pushing as hard as she could. The lights sparked to life first, followed by the music, and finally she'd nudged the platform forward. Once started, it was easier to increase the speed. She'd pushed her feet against the platform floor, trying to stand even as she pictured electrical energy pouring from her body into the platform and sending it whirling faster and faster.

The muscles in her legs trembled as she forced herself up, inch by inch, until her hands were level with the sharp, jagged hole cut by the ax. She shoved her wrists against the ragged edge, biting back a scream as the wood dug into her tender skin along with shredding the tape.

By the time Archie reached her, she was free. Free, but drained. Drained of the power to run the carousel and drained of the blood she had sacrificed to cut herself loose. Archie held one arm in a crushing grip while she batted him with the other, blood spraying on to the floor to match the blood already soaking into the raw gash on the horse's flank.

The platform was slowing, barely moving now, but Archie stumbled backward as if he'd hit an invisible wall. She yanked her arm free.

She had to run. But Archie had tied her ankles, and if she abandoned Gage, Archie would kill him. She tried to pry the tape around her legs free.

"Wake up," she yelled at Gage. "We have to get out of here."

"Let me help."

She looked up to see Archie holding his knife aloft.

"Get away from me."

He stepped closer and sliced through the tape holding her feet. She kicked at him, but he danced out of reach and pulled a gun from his pocket. "Try that again and I'll shoot you."

"Go ahead. Won't be the first time." She hopped off the platform and ran to Gage, drawing his head into her lap. His lips were blue.

"Hurts just as much the second time, but she wants to give you a choice."

"Resist her." Penny thought she felt Gage stir under her hands. *Please wake up.*

"You or him. Someone has to die here and you get to make the call."

"You're lying. You're going to kill both of us."

"Maybe." He grinned. "Maybe not."

Penny recalled her dream about the chieftain. How the man had willingly gone to his death to save his tribe. And she suddenly realized that's what Goldilocks wanted. She would accept blood of any type. But a sacrifice freely given was more valuable than one taken by force.

She lowered Gage's head gently to the floor and stood on wobbly legs. The horse knew she wouldn't allow Archie to kill Gage. She worried he had killed Plato. The little dog had done nothing but try to warn his owners of the danger. The dog's death would devastate Dora.

Dora.

Penny faltered, almost slipping back to the floor. Dora needed her. What would she do without her big sister looking out for her? "I can't."

"You choose him, then. Good call. He's probably not going to make it, anyway. But since I don't think you're going to just sit there and let me slit his throat, I'm going to have to tie you up again. Or maybe I'll just shoot you in the leg." He trained the gun on her.

She couldn't let Archie harm Gage. How would she go on without him? He had believed in her from the first day she'd walked into his cafe. Had promoted her to assistant manager. Sure, he had his crotchety moments and had blamed her unfairly for being jealous of his abilities, but no one was perfect.

"I won't let you hurt him."

Archie swung the gun towards Gage. "Don't know how you're going to stop me. She wants you, but she'll take what she's given."

Penny froze. The lasso around her heart tightened and tugged. The horse had fed on her before and wanted more. Penny wanted to help. She refused to turn into a monster like Archie, but she could still serve the ancient power. She only had to go willingly into the dark.

Dora would be all right. Gage, if he survived, would take care of her sister. He'd do it for Penny. And Dora had her own strength, forged in the accident's flame.

She stepped forward, bloody arms raised in surrender. "Take me."

Archie narrowed his eyes at her. Slowly, he turned the gun back towards her. He licked his lips. "Give me your arm."

Her arms felt heavy. One fell to her side as she extended the other. She blinked against the haze which fogged her mind. Was she going to allow this madman to kill her? Sacrifice her life for whatever lived inside the golden horse?

She snatched her hand back just before Archie took it. He growled and lunged at her.

No, she wasn't willing to die for the entity. But she would exchange her life for Gage's. Her death would even keep others safe. It would be a long time before Goldilocks needed a sacrifice again.

Her legs shook, but she allowed Archie to grab her. He didn't drag her onto the platform. She climbed up of her own accord. She kept her gaze focused on Goldilocks, not the knife Archie brandished.

The ragged gouge in the wood, smeared with her blood, had partially healed. The hole was shallower, smoother, and less jagged. Already the gift of her blood worked.

Archie plunged the blade into her forearm, slicing open the vein. She screamed, crumpling to the ground, the pain hot and burning along her already ravaged wrist. Blood poured from the wound, bright and crimson. Archie reached for her other arm, but this time instinct forced her to fight for her life. She batted at the knife, succeeding only in slicing open her palm, the blade tearing at the ridged, burn scar.

Anger flared along with the carousel lights. A bar of music played like a slow moan, and the platform lurched, causing Archie to stumble. He fell against the horse and she snorted, tapping her wooden hoof to the floor.

"Yes," Archie yelled, his eyes glazed with ecstasy. He reached for Penny again, but something crashed into him, taking him down to the ground.

Penny's vision wavered as she lay on the platform, her life leaking out, the smell of iron, sweat, and fear filling her nostrils. Gage. Gage was alive and fighting with Archie for control of the knife.

Her eyelids fluttered. Exhaustion dragged at her, pulling her under even as she urged her body to move, to join the fight against Archie. Gage yelled, and her heart tripped. Had Archie stabbed him? She wanted to look, but couldn't lift her head, couldn't do anything but stare at the blood pooling around her.

"Penny, listen to me. Hold on. Don't you give up."

She heard Gage's voice from far away, which was strange since they were only a few feet apart. He pressed something soft against her wound.

Stop the bleeding. Penny wasn't sure if the voice inside her head belonged to herself or Goldilocks. But surely the horse wouldn't want to lose her sacrifice. Her right arm weighed a ton, but she dragged it over and pressed her scarred, bloody palm against the knife wound.

Pain jolted through her, and she drifted away.

Chapter 22

Gradually Gage grew aware of his surroundings. He lay on a hard metal ridged surface, but couldn't move an inch. The surface was in motion, jolting him painfully against the ridges. Why couldn't he move?

He remembered taking the drug and stumbling into his closet. Then what? He vaguely recalled sinking into the earth, heat and pressure almost overwhelming him until he slipped into the coolness of a subterranean pool. He'd floated there, in bliss, until something pulled him under. Something dark, evil, and intent on drowning him.

He rattled over some bumps, his arms grinding against the metal. Plastic clung to his face, and he fought to breathe. A sharp turn sent his stomach into revolt. He was in a vehicle, in the back of a truck, he'd guess. Another turn. Something rolled against him, soft and warm. He tensed, but the object, another person he realized, didn't move. The scent of lavender shampoo teased his nostrils. Penny. He tried to move, but tape bound his arms and legs. Archie.

Where was he taking them? The carousel, most likely. Why? If Archie wanted to attack the ride again, why would he bring along those who had stopped him before? They weren't in any position to stop him this time, but why bring them along? To rub their faces in their defeat? Unfortunately, Gage thought something more ominous was in play.

He closed his eyes, tamped down his fear and concentrated. The image of the carousel formed in his mind. It was brightly lit, music playing, spinning around. All the animals were whole, and both children and adults rode, smiling and happy.

An image from the past or the future? Gage usually only saw what existed in the present or the very near future, such as when he'd seen the bomb at the Sunflower Showboat before it exploded. But the bomb had been there, ticking away. The carousel was not whole now. Archie had damaged it.

He delved deeper into the image, focusing on the golden horse Penny claimed was at the heart of the mysterious power the carousel held over her and the Jenkins family. It was a lovely piece of workmanship and in his vision he could see every stroke of the chisel and every drop of paint that had gone into making the creature incredibly lifelike. He could almost see the horse's mane flowing in the breeze and breath puffing from the horse's nostrils. And the eyes. They looked back at him, sentient and knowing.

Gage tried to shake his head, but it didn't move. Restraints chafed against his wrists. But something else held him still.

He gulped in air, feeling as if he were drowning. Logically, he knew the tarp pulled over their heads wasn't tight enough to suffocate them, but the fear didn't abate. Penny didn't move, and if it wasn't for the warmth of her body against his, he would have feared she was dead. What had Archie done to her? He suspected Archie had bound her as well, but he might have hurt her, too.

Drawing on the skills he'd learned at the agency, he forced his breathing to slow. His heart rate followed, and eventually he realized that although it was humid and musty under the tarp, there was enough air to breathe.

He tensed as the truck pulled to a stop. A car door slammed, and then someone lowered the tailgate. The tarp blocked his view, but someone, probably Archie, rustled around in the back, pulling items from the truck. The tailgate slammed shut again.

He heard footsteps, followed by silence. He heard nothing for several minutes but the rustle of small animals in the woods. After a while, he heard a single gunshot. What had happened? Had Archie killed someone? The park was extensive, but in a residential area. Would someone call the police?

Penny stirred. Gage sensed her panic as she struggled against her bonds, but couldn't speak. The drug locked his tongue as tightly as every other muscle in his body. When Archie returned to the truck, Gage listened helplessly while Penny called him out. When she mentioned Gage's name, he tried to give her a signal that he was aware, but she focused her attention on Archie.

It surprised him to hear her claim the horse was evil and suggest she and Archie destroy it together. She'd been under its thrall for the past several weeks. Had the carousel released its hold over her, or had Penny somehow broken free?

If he could have made a sound, he'd have groaned in frustration as Penny tried to reason with Archie's better nature. The man didn't have one. It surprised him when Archie actually hesitated, but almost before hope sparked, Archie doused it, blaming Gage for being a junkie. He wasn't wrong. Gage already suspected his paralysis came from the drug, rather than anything Archie had done to him. He prayed it would wear off soon.

When Archie slapped Penny, rage uncoiled within him. He could do nothing but lie there and watch Archie abuse his girlfriend. He fought against his bonds and, to his surprise, felt his fingers flutter. Curling and uncurling his fingers, he repeated the motion. He couldn't actually form a fist, but he could move.

Archie left the truck. A few moments later, Gage heard breaking glass. Footsteps announced Archie's return, but it still startled Gage when Archie yanked him by the feet and hauled him over his shoulder, firefighter style. He heard the man's panting as Archie struggled to carry him into the building. When they reached the carousel, Archie dumped him at the feet of the golden horse, just as he had threatened.

Archie reached for his neck and Gage braced himself, expecting the man's fingers to crush his windpipe and cut off his supply of oxygen. A tremor rippled through him when instead Archie merely pressed his fingers to his neck, apparently checking for a pulse.

Did he need to make sure his victim was still alive before he killed him? It made little sense unless Archie had planned something more elaborate than a simple murder. Gage's heart raced. He needed to get himself and Penny far away from this madman.

Out of the corner of his eye, he saw Archie coming for him with a knife. He could still barely move, and wondered if he would make a sound when Archie cut him. It took a few moments to realize Archie had cut the duct tape around his hands and feet, not his skin. Gage's limbs sprawled free, but he couldn't control them.

Archie left and returned with Penny. He threw her next to Gage. Gage wiggled his tongue, but couldn't form speech. When Archie moved towards him, knife at the ready, Gage tried to close his eyes. This was it. He'd wanted to regain his abilities. Wanted to help Penny. Instead, he would die trapped in his own body and she would follow. He should have taken her and Steve's advice. His impatience was going to cost them their lives.

He couldn't bear to look into Archie's gleeful gaze, but his eyelids merely fluttered, refusing to veil his sight.

Before the knife bit into his neck, the carousel flared to life. The lights came on, music rolled from the speakers, and the platform spun. Archie tripped, and the knife clattered to the ground. Gage gasped at the reprieve.

The carousel picked up speed, circling faster and faster. Gage's fingers scrambled for purchase, but found none. He bounced towards the edge and spun off, landing near the knife with a thud. The back of his head hit the floor, and pain arced through his skull.

As he lay on the ground, staring at the ceiling, his vision blurred and the brightly lit carousel faded. He saw a glass structure reflected in a pool of water. A fiery red glow lit the place from within. It crackled, moving sinuously, devouring all in its path. Hundreds of wings fluttered in panic. With a roar, the fire surged, and the glass shattered, sending thousands of iridescent crystals into the air. They rained down on the ground and into the water, creating tiny circles. Emboldened by the oxygen, the fire doubled in size, melting the metal bars holding the roof. Panes of glass fell, breaking, and triumphantly the fire shot straight up.

Could butterflies scream? It sounded as if they did. Even the plants seemed to cry out as the fire took hold. In the distance, more fires bloomed as the village also burned.

"Wake up! We have to get out of here."

Penny's voice broke through the vision, scattering it like a rock thrown into a pond. He blinked, saw the carousel, and realized his eyelids were working. He moved his hand, inching it towards the knife.

Long before he could reach it, Archie jumped off the carousel and scooped it off the floor. He paid no attention to Gage, but stared at Penny. When he cut her legs free, she ran straight for Gage and pulled his head into her lap. He pressed his head against her legs. Did she notice? It was the best he could do.

"You or him. Someone has to die here and you get to make the call."

Gage couldn't believe his ears. *Don't listen to him. Don't sacrifice yourself for me.*

"You're lying. You're going to kill both of us."

Smart girl. Fight him. Every step of the way.

"Maybe. Maybe not."

Penny slipped out from under him, placing his head gently on the floor. Gage wanted to howl in frustration. He tried to force his frozen muscles to move. Surely she wouldn't give her life for him. He was broken, wounded, and ten years her senior. She was youth and promise, her hair flaming as bright as the fire in his vision.

"I can't."

Air whooshed out of Gage's lungs. *Thank goodness she wasn't going through with it.*

"You choose him, then. Good call. He's probably not going to make it, anyway. But since I don't think you're going to just sit there and let me slit his throat, I'm going to have to tie you up again. Or maybe I'll just shoot you in the leg." He pointed the gun at Penny.

No. Gage fought his paralysis. One foot slithered across the floor.

Archie swung the gun back towards Gage. Had he seen Gage move?

"Don't know how you're going to stop me," Archie said.

Do it. Shoot me and let her go.

"Take me."

Gage wanted to scream at Penny to be quiet. Instead, he moved his other foot. He propped himself on his elbow and felt like he was the heavyweight champion of the year.

Penny screamed and the carousel sprang to life again, lights sparkling. Gage gathered himself and sprung, hitting the platform with one foot and barreling into Archie. They went down in a tumble. Gage slipped in blood. Penny's blood. It was all over the platform, way too much of it.

Archie swung the knife. Gage dodged, but it cut across his arm, drawing blood. He plunged his fist into Archie's soft belly. The other man grunted, but struck again with the knife. This time Gage wriggled clear, but when he reached for Archie's wrist, trying to disarm him, Archie cuffed him in the head with his other hand. Gage staggered and Archie drew the knife back again and plunged it towards Gage's shoulder.

At the last second, Gage shifted, and the knife skittered across his shoulder blade instead of digging home. He roared as hot pain sliced through him and attempted to knee Archie in the groin.

Archie twisted and although he took a solid blow to the thigh, he struggled to his feet, jumped off the platform and ran towards the door.

Gage crawled towards Penny. His arm and shoulder hurt, and his muscles still felt strange and uncooperative. He tore his bloody shirt over his head and pressed it to her bleeding wrist. "Penny, listen to me. Hold on. Don't you give up."

He could tell it took effort, but she dragged her other arm over and applied pressure to his shirt. He wanted to stay with her, to make sure she kept the pressure tight. When he had worked as part of a team at the agency, others had his back, but no one had ever offered their life for him. What she had done humbled him.

And frightened him to the core of his being.

He brushed the hair from her face. "Hold on. Help is coming." He fumbled for his phone. Dialed 911.

"There's been an accident. She's lost a lot of blood." He wasn't sure how to explain everything that was going on. "It's Archie Jenkins. The police are already looking for him, but he cut her and there's so much blood."

"Keep calm," the dispatcher said. "I'm sending the police and an ambulance. Stay on the line and keep pressure on the wound."

"I think he's going to blow up the Butterfly House."

There was a beat of silence. "Stay where you are. Officers are on their way."

He wanted to obey the dispatcher's orders. He wanted to stay with Penny. But he couldn't forget the sound of the screaming butterflies. Hundreds of them. Some rare and endangered.

"Please hurry." He stuffed the phone in his pocket and ran.

***

Gage and Archie were no longer there. Penny rolled into a fetal position, hugging her injured wrist to her chest. She'd lost a lot of blood, and her consciousness floated in and out. But Gage was okay. He'd regained his senses in time to keep Archie from making the second cut. Gritting her teeth against the pain, she pulled the blood stiffened tee shirt from her wound. The jagged line looked dreadful, red and angry, but the edges of the cut had seared shut and only a trickle of blood oozed out.

Feeling queasy, she wrapped the shirt back around her arm, tying it awkwardly with one hand. Why had Gage left her? She knew he'd called for help. He must have gone after Archie. She supposed he didn't want him to get away again, but she wished he would have stayed with her and left capturing Archie to the police. After attempting to murder them, Archie had very little left to lose. And desperate men were dangerous.

Penny drew herself up to her knees. The carousel appeared to sway, although she knew it was no longer moving. She had to stand, had to go after Gage. But she wanted nothing so much as to sink back onto the platform and wait for the sirens. Help would be there soon. But was it soon enough?

She heard a snort followed by the thud of a hoof hitting the platform. She looked up into the face of the golden horse, no longer made of wood, but alive in front of her.

"You wanted to kill me," she accused.

You have given me your blood.

The horse's eyes were intelligent. Knowing. Not that she was truly a horse. Penny knew the entity had merely taken on a recognizable form.

"You would have let him kill us."

Many things in life require sacrifice.

"You don't belong here. Not in the modern world."

And yet I am here.

"I have to find Gage."

Goldilocks stepped closer and nuzzled her.

Penny wrapped her arms around the animal's neck and dragged herself to her feet. Again, the room swayed.

You saw me in your dreams.

Penny recalled the horses she'd ridden, the surreal dream about the carousel, and the final disturbing one with the sacrifice. If she accepted the creature's help, would she be binding them closer together than they already were?

"Why me?"

"*Your blood was strong. I knew it from the first taste. And the caretaker's son is... unpredictable.*"

Penny almost walked away. But if she did, she would fall flat on her face. She had given this creature her blood. By accident and on purpose. They would always be linked. She stepped into the stirrup and swung up onto the horse's back. "Go."

The horse took off. Penny ducked as they crashed through the gaping hole in the window where Archie had carved out an opening. She raised her head as they hit the parking lot. The sun peeped over the horizon, bathing the world in a rosy glow, but it wasn't the glow of the sun which caught her eye. The village, comprising historical properties brought to the park from throughout the state, was alight. Flames licked up the old wood and had already jumped to at least one tree. There were neighborhoods nearby. How long would it take the fire to spread to them?

"You don't want this, right? Hundreds dying while supposedly safe in their beds?"

Goldilocks danced in place, hooves clattering on the blacktop. Her ears were back, her eyes wild. It was invigorating. Electrifying. Even Penny could feel the leashed power in the air. It had to be so tempting.

No.

Penny squeezed her knees, and they were off, tearing across the parking lot and into the field. She searched for Gage and Archie but saw no one. Past the village was the paddock where the horses lived. Their neighs of terror carried over the crackling of the hungry flames. Goldilocks heard them too. She might not be an actual horse, but she wasn't unaffected. Tension thrummed beneath her golden coat and she responded, shrill with command.

Sirens roared in the distance, and Penny took a deep breath, choking on the smoke. Help was on the way. She only hoped the fire department would arrive in time to save some of the history, besides people's homes.

Her eyes watered. Where were Gage and Archie? Would she even be able to see them if she found them? What if they were inside one of the buildings?

A pop sounded as something exploded. Wood cracked and split. Penny whirled Goldilocks around to the sound, expecting to see the building in pieces, but it still stood. Goldilocks whinnied, tossing her head. Penny followed her line of sight. A horse had kicked through the paddock fence and was leading the others to safety.

She and Goldilocks completed their circuit of the village with no sign of Gage or Archie. Penny headed for the park entrance, planning to direct emergency services towards the flaming village. But as the rays of dawn hit the glass of the Butterfly House, making it sparkle like a diamond, she glimpsed the fire burning deep inside. Suddenly she knew where Gage and Archie were.

She dug her heels into Goldilocks' flanks, and they raced towards the greenhouse. Archie had started the blaze, but Gage must have caught him before it fully caught. Unlike the village, which might not be salvageable, the Butterfly House, and the butterflies within it, might still survive.

Gage and Archie struggled in the entrance, their figures silhouetted by the smoldering fire within. Cans of gasoline were scattered around. One had rolled dangerously close to the flames.

Penny didn't hesitate. Archie looked up, eyes widening in terror as the living embodiment of the entity which had influenced his life bore down on him. He had tried to resist her, damage her, and seize control from her. She wasn't in the mood for forgiveness. Neither was Penny. As they thundered towards the pair, Penny kicked out at Gage, shoving him clear. Then they crashed into Archie and he went down, flesh rending under iron-shod hooves. He didn't even have time to scream.

Penny jumped down from the horse and ran to Gage. Her kick had sent him sprawling, but he regained his feet before she reached him. She threw herself into his arms, which closed tightly around her.

"I thought you were dead."

Gage swung her up against the glass wall, pressed his body against her, and ravished her mouth. Penny could barely breathe by the time he lifted his head.

"I'm sorry. I took the potion to help you, but it nearly got you killed. Whatever were you thinking to offer yourself to Archie? I'm not worth it."

That he so clearly believed what he was saying made the sacrifice more than worth it to Penny. She felt she'd been waiting most of her life for someone to put her first. Not that Ben wasn't brave or didn't care about her. She knew he did. He'd risked his life to save hers when the sniper pinned them down. But he didn't look at her the way Gage did. Didn't understand her the way Gage did. For all that he was a talented medium, Ben was a ray of light in the darkness. A hint of darkness lived inside Gage, as it did Penny. It was something she hoped Ben would never fully understand.

"Of course, you're worth it, but next time listen to me, you stupid oaf." She punched him in the arm. "I couldn't go on if you weren't here to help me."

Gage pulled her close again, gently this time, tucking her head under his neck. They still stood there, clinging to one another, when the authorities arrived.

One firetruck had come with the first responders as a matter of course, but soon the entire fleet, as well as trucks from neighboring communities, arrived.

Thanks to Gage, they put out the blaze in the Butterfly House almost immediately, losing only a few butterflies, most of which escaped through a hole in the glass. The rest of the fire trucks thundered towards the village to save what they could.

A paramedic placed a sheet over Archie. Penny heard a police officer call for the medical examiner.

"We need to question the witnesses."

The EMT who was treating Gage and Penny refused to give them access. "You can question them at the hospital after they're stabilized."

The policeman looked unhappy about the delay, but the scene was chaos. Some horses had fled, but others milled around, snorting nervously. With the gruesome evidence of what they could do covered by a sheet, most of the personnel kept their distance from the animals.

Penny looked around for Goldilocks, but didn't see her. The horse had probably returned to the carousel and once again assumed her inanimate existence. It was for the best. How would she explain a living carousel horse?

When the paramedics placed an oxygen cup over her face, the police wandered away. She would have some time to think of a coherent story, keeping as close to the truth as possible without talking about mysterious entities and human sacrifice.

The paramedics lifted their stretchers into the ambulance, and she and Gage held hands as they sped towards the hospital.

Archie had died. The goddess, for Penny felt sure Goldilocks considered herself a goddess, had gotten her sacrifice. Would it be enough? Penny wasn't sure, but she hoped the events of the evening had broken her connection to the entity. Any debt she owed to Goldilocks, she had paid in full.

Chapter 23

T he radio kicked over to a new song, and Penny smiled as
Adam's melodious voice carried through the backyard. Adam
had agreed to let Jackson write some songs for East of Eden's new
album, and this one was a breakout hit. Penny would have liked the
song anyway, but since she felt involved in its creation, it had become
one of her all-time favorites. Jackson was also writing songs for his own
band, Hyperbolic.

Her injuries were healing. The bullet wound on her arm quickly
healed once she stopped straining it. The electrical burn on her wrist
was still painful, although she supposed it had saved her life. She was
under strict orders not to return to work for another week.

The park department had apologized to her and told her she could
have the carousel job back, but Penny had turned them down. She
still felt a connection to Goldilocks, but it lacked urgency. Perhaps
the horse had gotten so much power from Archie's death, she didn't
feel the need for a caretaker. Penny only hoped she would be strong
enough to resist Goldilocks' call if it came again.

Penny was going back to work at the cafe, although she might continue to look for another job, since she wasn't sure working with her
boyfriend was good for their relationship. The newspapers portrayed
her and Gage as heroes, saying if they hadn't stopped Archie when

they did, he would have burned down the Butterfly House in addition to the damage he'd done to the carousel and village.

Some of the village was still standing, although none of the buildings were unscathed. Archaeologists were already hard at work restoring what they could. Some buildings had suffered too much damage and the park service tore them down. They debated about whether to construct copies, but the originals were gone forever.

The Butterfly House was also under repair, but the damage done to it was minor compared to what Gage had seen in his vision. Whenever Penny saw a butterfly visit their small flower garden, she wondered if it could be one of the few that had escaped. It made her happy to think they were free, even though she knew they had a lovely habitat in the greenhouse with all the food they needed and where they lived protected from the dangers present in the wild.

Dishes clattered as Dora brought out a tray with cake and lemonade. Gage followed with a bag of sandwiches from the cafe. Gage had only left her side to deal with restaurant business, and Dora had been waiting on her hand and foot. What had first seemed to be an incredible luxury was becoming a nuisance.

Her heart thumped with joy as Plato limped out with them. She'd thought for sure she would never see the little dog again, but his recovery wasn't the only medical miracle. The hospital staff had stared at the partially cauterized wound on her wrist with disbelief. She didn't think they accepted her explanation. She'd told them the carousel had been malfunctioning, that the lights, music, and motion had gone on and off at random. The investigators had found a loose cable and theorized it caused the trouble. They stated it must have overheated and transferred enough heat to the platform to burn her wrist, halting the flow of blood.

It was as good an explanation as any and Penny wondered if the loose cable had enabled her to access the ride's electronics. It seemed she no longer needed direct contact to harness the power of electricity.

She reached for Plato and gently pulled the dog into her lap. Her wrists were still a mess and would probably always bear the scars of that night. She'd scraped both of them while trying to saw her hands free and while the cuts were healing, they were still red and raw. Her left wrist, with the deep gash along her vein, overlaid with a burn, ached fiercely.

"Tell Gage what happened with Plato," she said to Dora.

Dora poured them each a glass of lemonade, and Gage handed out sandwiches. She sat and tapped her fingers on the table. "He knows about your crystal ball?"

Penny nodded.

"Our great-grandmother gave each of us a gift. Mine was a healing ointment. I didn't hear Archie break in since I was asleep and without my hearing aid. But after he left, Plato dragged himself upstairs and into my room. He woke me."

She paused and took a sip of lemonade. "He was covered in blood. I ran to Penny's room, but she wasn't there. Her shoes rested by the bed and I found her phone on the floor. I didn't think she left willingly and guessed Archie was responsible."

"I wasn't sure what to do first. I needed to notify the police about Penny's disappearance, but Plato was dying right before my eyes. In the end, I thought it best to rush him to the animal hospital and call the police from there. I wasn't even sure they would do anything since Penny hadn't been missing for more than a couple hours and other than her phone on the floor, there really weren't any signs of a struggle."

Plato had perked his ears at the mention of his name, and he gave a soft whine deep in his throat. Penny passed him on to Dora.

"As I wrapped Plato in a blanket, his heart stopped. I'm not sure how I knew it. I'm studying physical therapy in school, but I'm not a vet or a doctor. But I knew I didn't have enough time to take him anywhere. Then I remembered the ointment."

She stroked Plato, careful not to touch his incision. "We received our inheritances on our sixteenth birthdays. Since then I've followed instructions, telling no one the secret formula, and making a fresh batch every three months. I've used it on myself, particularly after the car accident, but although it made my wounds heal faster, it did nothing to restore my hearing. I put some on Penny's burn when she got shocked on the Sunflower.

"I grabbed it, smeared some on the bullet hole and began CPR. School hasn't trained me to do it on an animal, but I tried to copy what I would do for a person, making adjustments for Plato's smaller size."

"She got his heart going, just as she did with Mr. Jenkins," Penny said when Dora fell silent. Her sister had a faraway look in her eyes as if she saw something other than their lunch and the sun-dappled shade of their backyard.

"I restarted his heart and his bleeding seemed to slow, but that might have been because he had already lost so much blood. I drove him to the nearest twenty-four-hour animal hospital and as soon as they rushed him into surgery, I called the police."

Penny took over the story. "They didn't want to listen to her. They said they had to wait until I'd been missing for forty-eight hours. As an adult, I was free to take off in the middle of the night without my shoes or phone if I wanted to. In her panic, Dora didn't notice the back door had been broken.

"But Dora kept pushing and when she told them about the shooting and the vandalism at the carousel, they took things more seriously. Finally, they agreed to notify local police and have them swing by the park. The patrol officer spotted the fire in the village and got emergency personnel there quicker than they would have otherwise. We might have lost the entire village if not for her."

Dora's shoulders slumped. "But if I'd called them first, Archie might not have cut you. You almost died because of my delay."

Penny shook her head. "If the police had arrived earlier, before Archie set the fire, they might not have noticed anything wrong unless they specifically checked the carousel building. And Plato would have died for sure."

"He's a dog. You're my sister."

Penny reached across the table and took Dora's hand. "He's a member of our family. I was heartbroken when I thought we had lost him."

Dora squeezed Penny's hand before releasing it to dash a tear from her cheek. "You didn't even want him at first."

"I changed my mind." And not just about the dog. Even though she wasn't looking at Gage, she could feel his warm and steady presence beside her. She'd tried with Ben, but would try even harder with Gage now that she realized how much he meant to her.

"I forgot to bring a knife for the cake," Dora said. She set Plato down. "I'll be right back."

Since they hadn't even finished their sandwiches, Penny suspected it was an excuse to either give her some time alone with Gage or to allow Dora to collect her emotions.

"The police have closed their investigation," Gage said. "They will file no charges against you."

Penny supposed the news should relieve her. After all, she had killed someone, although he'd tried to kill her and Gage first. "That's great."

"It was a straightforward case of self-defense."

Was it? Penny wasn't so sure. Her life had not actually been in jeopardy when she rode him down. Gage's maybe, but not hers. She also wasn't sure she could have stopped Goldilocks even if she'd wanted to. Archie had broken the long-standing agreement between the entity and his family. She'd been hot for revenge.

"I rode Goldilocks," Penny said. She'd allowed the police to believe she'd ridden one of the park horses, but wanted Gage to know the truth.

Gage massaged her shoulders. "You almost died. You were low on blood and probably in shock. I think your mind played tricks on you."

"I know what happened." She shrugged off his hands.

"If you're sure, I believe you. We've seen some very weird stuff. But you also told me that the wood somehow knitted itself back together. The gash is still there, although the park has vowed to repair it, along with the faulty cable and busted lights."

"I can't explain why the damage disappeared and then returned. Maybe it was just an illusion."

"The important thing is that you're now free of its influence."

Penny nodded, not wanting Gage to know she could still feel the horse's presence. She had considered recommending the park not repair Goldilocks and replace it with another animal. But in the end, she hadn't been able to do it. She convinced herself it would be a long time before the goddess required fresh blood.

"And you will not overdose on experimental potions anymore?"

"No, but I am going to continue treatment. I admit I was stupid. I was in too much of a hurry. But this is important to me."

"Let's make a deal. I won't allow myself to be bossed around by ancient evil entities and you won't forgo all safety protocols."

"Deal." They bumped fists.

The back door snapped open, and Dora appeared with the knife. She dished out the cake and regained her seat.

"Penny, I've been thinking. I'm finally ready to see Dad in person. Next Sunday is Father's Day. I think we should go visit him together."

***

Tidbits:

1. The carousel in *The Wheel of Misfortune* is based on a real carousel. It was built in 1921 by the Dentzel Company.

2. Forest Park Highlands purchased the carousel and installed it in 1929.

3. In 1963 fire destroyed the amusement park. The fire started in a cooking area. As far as I know, arson was never suspected.

4. The carousel survived and was donated to the St. Louis Department of Parks and Recreation in 1965.

5. The carousel operated in Sylvan Springs Park until 1979.

6. It was later restored to its original beauty and moved to Faust Park in 1987.

7. Faust Park is also home to the Butterfly House, a greenhouse with nearly 2000 butterflies.

8. Several old buildings have also been moved to Faust Park to preserve them from destruction.

Mother's Day turned out to be a bust. Will Father's Day be any better? Find out by reading The Lost Cave.

Connect with me:
Email: clpeper@charter.net
Website: https://cathypeper.com/
Facebook: https://www.facebook.com/CathyPeper.author

Sign up for my newsletter and receive a Free prequel short story to the *In for a Penny* series and news about upcoming releases.

Please Review:

I hope you enjoyed *The Wheel of Misfortune*. Please consider leaving a review so other readers, like yourself, can find books they like. Click here:

Other Books by Cathy Peper

Wings and Arrows: A Forbidden Love Paranormal Romance Serial

Wings and Arrows part 1 of 6

Wings and Arrows part 2 of 6

Wings and Arrows part 3 of 6

Wings and Arrows part 4 of 6

Wings and Arrows part 5 of 6

Wings and Arrows part 6 of 6

The Blue Crystal Adventures:

Time Shattering

Time Rebound

Stowaway in Time

Meet me in Time

Regency Romances:

The Seventh Season

Peyton and the Paragon

In for a Penny Paranormal Suspense:

The Haunting of Sycamore House

The Lady in Red

The Wheel of Misfortune:

The Lost Cave

The Dream Stealer

About the Author

Cathy Peper lives in the Midwest with her husband and three college-aged children. A lifelong reader, she is now enjoying her lifelong dream of being an author and bringing the stories she loves to read to other readers. In the rare moments when it's not too hot, too cold, or raining, you might find her bicycling to the winery to kick back, relax and drink wine.

Made in the USA
Las Vegas, NV
22 April 2024

88985124R00142